# SPELLBOUND

## MAGIC & MECHANICALS BOOK 5

### JESSICA MARTING

SHADOW PRESS

# SPELLBOUND

# CHAPTER 1

*30 September 1889*

*Dear Mr. Sloan,*

*I understand you offer discreet private investigation services and would like to hire you as soon as possible. I can pay handsomely. I will match the sum paid by any other client who would otherwise engage you. The matter is dear to my heart, concerning the untimely death of my father and the woman he married who has since found herself in possession of his fortune since that unfortunate event.*

*I eagerly await your response at your earliest convenience.*

*Sincerely,*

*Ezra Thaddeus*

Merritt Sloan kept his expression schooled in what he hoped was neutral at the display before him. The couple sitting across the table truly were disgusting in their affection for each other.

Newlyweds Ben and Elora Lang, vampire and

vampire's mate, sat across the table from him. Wax candles in brass holders and a bottle of red wine rested in the middle of the table. Their chairs were pushed together closer than would be considered polite in English society, their fingers intertwined. If Elora's pearl engagement ring hadn't been visible, Merritt wouldn't have known whose fingers belonged to who.

And the *looks* they kept giving each other! Even the other restaurant patrons had noticed, with the occasional raised eyebrow sent in their direction, quickly followed by a whispered comment to a supper companion. Ben looked at Elora like he was ready to eat her at the table, manners be damned, and Merritt supposed he would feed off her later in the night. The high collar of Elora's dark blue evening dress barely hid a healing puncture mark in her neck.

As it was, the plates of food in front of Merritt and Elora had barely been touched. Merritt looked at his rapidly cooling roast beef in front of him and sighed. It smelled divine. He didn't know which would be more rude: eating before Elora picked up her spoon or wolfing it down the way he wanted to.

Merritt cleared his throat.

Ben pulled away from Elora's ear, where he'd been whispering something undoubtedly filthy in it. "Beg your pardon," he said, trying to hide a smile.

"How are you finding your return to England? Where are you staying?" The pair had been traveling around Europe for over a year and recently returned. Merritt had made the weekend trip out to London specifically to see them while they were still visiting.

"We've rented a flat in Marylebone for our stay," Elora replied. "Its windows have blackout drapes and the other tenants leave us alone. It reminds us a bit of our first flat in

Italy." The pair of them shared a look that spoke volumes in a language only they could understand.

Oh, this was bordering on intolerable. He eyed his plate and tried not to be irritated by the untouched meal on it, taunting him.

"What are you up to, then?" Ben asked when he finally tore his gaze away from his wife. "You're one of the only people we wanted to see after we returned. How is life treating you? You said in your last letter that you stopped your police work."

Merritt shifted, unsure how to approach the question. He may as well be honest. "I was never a policeman."

Both of them stared at him. "What?" Elora asked.

Merritt cleared his throat. "It was easier to pass myself off as one when I was investigating vampire massacres and other supernatural crimes. I'm a private detective who occasionally used to do consulting work with the Liverpool constabulary when they needed help." He considered his next words, hoping they wouldn't judge him too badly about them. "My methods produce results but they aren't always ethical."

Elora slowly nodded. "So, they could find out who the murderers are for a particular case without having to concern themselves with following procedures."

Relief flooded through Merritt at her reaction. He hadn't realized how nervous he was about them ending their fragile friendship due to his dishonesty. "Yes, although I'm no longer doing that. I'm strictly working for myself these days. In fact, I have a new case I'll be starting on Tuesday morning."

"Another wayward vampire?" Elora asked, picking up her fork.

Oh, thank God. Merritt thought she would never eat. He cut a piece of roast beef and ate it before answering.

When he did, he chose his words carefully, mindful of the other diners. "No. I have yet to be hired to investigate a case involving our kind of people."

Evidently, he hadn't picked his words thoughtfully enough. Ben and Elora tilted their heads to the side, eager to hear Merritt's secrets about what he truly was. He knew they suspected he wasn't fully human. Merritt had kept that part of himself private.

He ate another mouthful of food, stalling.

"Come on," Ben said, voice soft. He leaned forward. "What the hell are you?"

"Mostly human, same as you."

"We've trusted you with our secrets. You're the only person other than my parents and brother we've looked up since we came back to London. You can trust us."

"I'm certain I could. It's other vampires I wouldn't trust."

Elora's gaze flicked between both men. She picked up her wine glass and took a cautious sip. "We only know one other vampire and you've met her already. None of us are going to give you up to a group of bad ones."

Merritt had never revealed what he was to others. A part of him ached to do so, to relieve that burden of being what he was off his shoulders. He looked away for a moment, at another group of diners laughing at something. An unexpected pang of loneliness pricked at him like an erroneous stickpin. They looked happy. So did the couple across the table from him. Merritt was always alone, unless the dead came to bother him. The truly dead, not the vampire sharing his table.

Ben and Elora had to be a decade younger than him, but they were the closest things in his life that he had to friends. Friends didn't keep these kinds of secrets from one another. "Necromancer," he said quietly.

"I'm sorry?" Ben said.

Was it because he'd been too quiet or because Ben didn't know what a necromancer was? "I'm a necromancer," Merritt replied. "Courtesy of my fae lineage a few generations back."

Ben and Elora stared at him for a few seconds, aghast. "Fae? Do you have wings?" Ben finally asked.

Merritt stared at him. "Wings? Are you serious? I just told you that I can speak to spirits and you want to know if I have fucking *wings*?"

"Well, now that you've phrased it like that, I certainly feel like an idiot." The import of Merritt's confession finally seemed to sink in. "Can you raise the dead?"

He shuddered at the question. Unpleasant memories rose and he quickly tamped them down. "I'm better at speaking to spirits."

"Could you raise a group of sleeping vampires?" Elora asked.

He'd never tried and never would. "Possibly, and I don't want them to know there's someone out there who can do that," Merritt whispered. "I'm sure you can see the danger it would put me in. I have no desire to bother any of you, as long as you aren't eating people." Elora gave him a withering look. "Without their permission," Merritt hastily added. "I really have nothing to say about your arrangement if it makes you happy."

"Are your abilities why you're a detective?" she asked.

"Yes."

"That laboratory in Liverpool?" Ben prompted.

He nodded. "But for every case involving a mermaid or vampire, there's a couple dozen garden-variety murder cases I'm hired to investigate. It's remarkable what one can accomplish when a spirit can be summoned to tell me who killed him. I've been hired for such a case that I'll start investigating tomorrow afternoon, as a matter of fact, not that I believe it was murder."

"Why not?" Ben leaned forward again, intrigued, as Elora dug into her meal.

"It's a high profile case. I don't suppose you've heard of Dr. Thaddeus's Miracle Elixir?"

Elora snorted but didn't respond. Merritt didn't blame her. The patent medicine bearing Dr. Thaddeus's name was a harmless but expensive fraud.

"There's a dispute over the rights of the late Dr. Thaddeus's estate and his manner of death," Merritt said. "His son has hired me to look into his death. He believes his stepmother killed his father."

"Did she?" Ben asked.

"I'll have to go to Dr. Thadddeus's house to summon him and ask. I doubt it, though. Dr. Thaddeus was in his late sixties when he died. His son has admitted he was in poor health and under the care of a physician. I believe this is likely a case of a child disgruntled that he was passed over in his father's will for his stepmother, who by all rights is entitled to the estate anyway."

"Then why take on the case if you already know what happened?"

"Ezra Thaddeus is paying me five hundred pounds to investigate. To me, that's a lot of money." Elora's eyes widened at the sum. It was a lot of money to her, too. Merritt knew she was the formerly destitute sister of a duke who had disowned her.

"In that case, you can pay for our supper next time," Ben said.

"I'd be happy to pay for it this evening."

Ben shook his head. "We invited you out. Will you be investigating in London?"

"The Thaddeus estate is just outside Liverpool city

limits. I'll fly back tomorrow morning." Elora faintly shuddered at the mention of flight and Merritt bit back a smile. She hated heights and flying.

"So, you'll fly to the estate, speak to Dr. Thaddeus's kindly old widow, speak to the dead man's ghost, and take five hundred pounds from his son? That's a profitable racket," Ben said.

"It's hardly a racket. It's a curse I'm forced to live with. I may as well make some money off it." Merritt had taught himself to ignore the wayward spirits who recognized what he was and tried to talk to him, but that didn't make being pestered by them any easier.

"That's a rather mercenary way to look at it, but I can't say I disapprove." Ben picked up the untouched wineglass in front of him and held it up in a toast.

"You're not serious," Merritt said.

"I am." He nudged Elora, who picked up hers. With a sigh, Merritt did likewise. "Here I was, thinking you were a paragon of morals, keeping England safe from monsters like me. Instead, you're bilking the estates of lonely old widows and grieving sons. Is it wrong that I'm proud of you?"

"My God," Elora said.

Merritt knew his expression had to match the awestruck tone in her voice. Merritt didn't bother to hide his eye roll. "To the decay of morals," he said, touching the lip of his glass against Ben's.

Ivy Thaddeus's wards were failing. She bit back a scream of frustration, forcing her voice to a whisper as she recited another spell. She could only hope that this one would work and Ezra would finally give up and leave. Her words were breathless, barely audible as if she was afraid he could hear her casting the spell through the heavy front door he beat with his fists. She finished the incantation and waited. The air shifted, as if acknowledging her spell, and she let out a watery breath.

Ezra's pounding at the door ceased. He'd lost interest in harassing her, at least for the night.

Ivy crept along the darkened foyer to the window next to the door. She watched as Ezra sauntered down the cobblestone path back to his waiting carriage as if he hadn't just been spelled away. It was a temporary reprieve. She had no illusions that he wouldn't be back in the morning with the private investigator he told her he hired.

Under ordinary circumstances, Ivy would have been able to cast a spell that would repel the investigator, but her magic was inexplicably fading fast. Perhaps it would be easiest to give up and cede the entire estate to Ezra.

She shook her head as if to dislodge the thought. No, she couldn't give up the estate. It was her home. Ezra had received a significant settlement, greater than the value of the house, and it should be enough for him.

She wiped tears from her eyes and mentally tallied up every protection spell she hadn't tried yet. The list was short and getting shorter with each passing day as her magic faded, joining her husband in death.

# CHAPTER 2

MERRITT DOUBLE CHECKED his pockets to ensure his notebook and pencil were still where they should be before slipping out of his ornithopter's passenger basket. He had landed the vehicle where Ezra Thaddeus told him to, at the foot of the Thaddeus family estate. A wide cobblestone pathway led to a large, nondescript brick house at the top of a hill. It didn't have any of the trappings of the excessively wealthy that he would have expected from someone like Dr. Thaddeus.

The steady clip-clop of horse hooves against the hard-packed earth beneath them had Merritt tearing his gaze away from the house. A pair of the beasts hauled a small carriage behind them. As it came into view, Merritt saw the man holding the reins wasn't much younger than his thirty-one years. A breeze nearly pulled his hat from his head and the man gripped its brim with one hand, the reins gathered in the other before he indicated the horses should stop.

Merritt waited until the man alighted from the carriage. His clothes were too fine to be that of the house's staff, despite driving himself, and his walk was too self-assured. It was the gait of a man who was used to getting his way, a type of person Merritt was all too familiar with after working as a detective for as long as he had.

"Mr. Sloan," the man said by way of greeting. He held out his hand.

"Pleasure to meet you." Merritt accepted the greeting and shook the proffered hand, noting the firm grip.

"Ezra Thaddeus. Thank you for traveling all the way here." The younger man looked over the ornithopter, a glimmer of appreciation in his blue eyes. "I trust your trip was pleasant?"

"As pleasant as it can be in an open top ornithopter. There's never a shortage of insects to join you in the skies."

Ezra smiled wanly at the remark. "I've considered purchasing one for my own use, although my father discouraged it. Said they were too dangerous."

Speaking of the late Dr. Thaddeus… Merritt hadn't felt the man's spirit since he landed, nor any other spirits, which was surprising. There was usually one or two about these kinds of properties, the ghosts of past residents or servants who simply didn't want to leave. They left everyone still alive alone, preferring to spend their afterlives among the house or gardens they'd enjoyed and tended to before they died. The silence at this place was unnerving. It was as if the dead had been banished from the property. He looked up at the house perched at the top of the hill and a faint shudder rippled through him. Merritt shook off the feeling. He grasped on to the late doctor's name and steered the conversation toward him. "Shall we start the investigation? I'd like to take a look at the house."

"I appreciate your forthrightness." Something sparkled in Ezra's eye, but Merritt couldn't read it.

They started the walk up the cobblestone path. It was a

treacherous design choice, probably to deter wayward travelers from trying to steer horses or steam cabs to the house. As it was, Merritt had trouble keeping his balance along the stones and moved at a slower pace behind Ezra. The air shifted as they ascended, causing goosebumps to pop up along his skin. An odd sense of dread overcame him, along with the urge to flee. Still, he forged on, catching up to Ezra whose expression was pinched. Merritt wondered if he felt the change, too.

There was something unearthly in that house, and damned if he could put his finger on what it was.

Merritt had five hundred pounds on the line if he ran away now. Steeling himself, he forced his feet to move along the cobblestones to match Ezra's pace. A large brass and iron knocker in the shape of a Celtic cross decorated the heavy front door, another unusual design choice. Who used iron to protect their house in this day and age? Merritt already knew the answer. Someone superstitious, who wanted to keep out creatures like himself. If he'd been fully fae, he wouldn't have been able to venture further to the house, but his human side was unaffected by it.

A curtain twitched in the window next to the door, but Merritt couldn't see anything or anyone else.

He didn't need to. A wave of nausea crested over him as they walked closer to the house and he swallowed, tamping it down. His original estimation of the case ahead of him and the stepmother at the center of it immediately changed. The sense of dread as he walked along the cobblestones, coupled with the iron knocker weren't coincidences. He wasn't dealing with grieving relatives fighting over a patent medicine fortune, but something far more sinister.

Ezra Thaddeus had hired him to investigate a witch.

Merritt was dizzy on his feet when they reached the

front door and Ezra pounded on it with his fist. He breathed deeply, calling on his human side to hold him up in the face of iron and witch's protection spells. They weren't very strong; if they had been, Ezra and Merritt wouldn't have been able to step foot on the property. The spell's effects were more annoying than anything else. Merritt knew that once he left the property, his breathing and constitution would return to normal.

"She changed the locks," Ezra said when he beat the door again. "I swear to God that one of these days I shall simply knock down the door."

The door unexpectedly opened, revealing a darkened foyer. A woman stepped out of the shadows to face them. Her full lips were pursed into a scowl. "Why are you here?" she asked by way of greeting. "Who is this?"

The air around her seemed to sizzle with electricity. Power radiated from her, touching something in Merritt, searing a part of himself that he kept hidden from the world. His nausea evaporated, replaced by surprise.

"I told you I would be hiring someone to investigate my father's death," Ezra replied coolly. "This is Merritt Sloan, private detective for hire. Mr. Sloan, this is my stepmother, Ivy Wickham Thaddeus."

She certainly wasn't what Merritt had been expecting. He was still surprised to see that this was the evil stepmother, a woman decades younger than the late Dr. Thaddeus. Her dark hair was swept into a chignon at the base of her neck. Her gray and lavender half-mourning dress impeccable in style and condition. Her green eyes examined Merritt closely, narrowing at him in suspicion. He nodded at her out of politeness. "Madam." His voice was even, emotionless.

She knew there was something otherworldly about him, just as he knew that about her.

Part of him wanted to toss aside the case, tell Ezra to stuff his five hundred pounds and leave the property immediately. A witch could be a powerful foe, even if her protection spells could be stepped over like hers were. That didn't mean she didn't have a whole host of tricks and wards that could be used in other ways. He reminded himself that he had his own tricks. It might be more difficult than usual, but he could still summon her dead husband's spirit, be directed somewhere or to something that would implicate his wife in his death.

"I told you there was no reason to involve the police," Mrs. Thaddeus said, tone sharp.

"I'm a private detective, not a policeman," Merritt replied, cutting off Ezra before he could speak.

"I fail to see the difference. Every physician who has examined your father's body determined his death to be of natural causes. There is no need for a private detective." Ivy's spine straightened. "I'll ask both of you to leave now."

"This is my father's house," Ezra snapped. "I still have the right to enter it."

"It's *my* house and you will do no such thing."

Except they could. Merritt could feel her protection spell breaking apart like dandelion seeds on the wind. Judging by the way her lips thinned, she could feel it, too. He and Ezra could simply waltz into the home as if they owned the place, if they wanted to.

Ezra's demeanor relaxed and he crossed the threshold. Mrs. Thaddeus sighed in frustration, and for a second her eyes shone with tears. Just as quickly, she blinked and her expression returned to that of cool irritation.

She was scared of her stepson.

Ezra turned around to face Merritt, who remained

outside. "Come on," he said. "Let's start this investigation."

Ivy flinched, a barely perceptible movement. Her green eyes caught Merritt's, and he could have sworn he saw a pleading look reflected there, but it wasn't for him to leave. She needed help.

What the hell had he gotten himself into?

Holding back a frustrated sigh, Merritt walked into the house.

WHAT IN ALL the names of all the gods and goddesses was this man? Had Ezra discovered what she was and sought out a supernatural private detective to expose her?

"This is one of the finest detectives in England," he announced. She hated the smugness in his tone and would have slapped it had it been tangible. "He has an uncanny knack for uncovering clues overlooked by subpar detectives and policemen. Isn't that right, Sloan?"

"I certainly try," the detective said. His dark eyes flitted around the foyer, taking in every detail.

"You'll need to do better than merely trying to prove that my father's wife killed him."

Ire and rage rose within her at the accusation, as they always did when Ezra threw those words at her. "I did not. His heart failed. You know that." To Mr. Sloan, she said, "I'll show you the reports from the doctors who autopsied him. There wasn't anything in his body to suggest that he died from anything other than a weak heart."

"I take it Dr. Thaddeus didn't try his own patent medicine?" Mr. Sloan quipped.

"Of course he did," Ivy replied. "He believed in the

power of his medicines. Unfortunately, a weak heart isn't a condition his Miracle Elixir could have cured."

"So, calling it a 'miracle' tonic is false advertising." Mr. Sloan removed a small leather-bound notebook and pencil from his trousers pocket. "How long has it been since your husband passed away, Mrs. Thaddeus?"

She itched to slap him for that remark, but kept her hands at her sides. Was he truly intending to interrogate her in her own foyer? "We aren't doing this," she said evenly. "Both of you need to leave. I don't see *why* you're doing this, Ezra. You've received almost everything else from your father."

"You will cooperate with Mr. Sloan and I'll consider sitting down to negotiations with you and your solicitor," Ezra replied.

Ivy blinked in surprise. She hadn't been expecting that. "You'll leave me be if I allow Mr. Sloan access to my house?"

"It's my father's house, and I said I would consider negotiations with you if you let him complete his investigation." He stiffened. "Although I doubt I'll have to, once Mr. Sloan proves that you murdered my father and you're hanged for it."

Mr. Sloan visibly blanched at the threat. His eyes met hers, and she thought she saw a shred of sympathy there. She seized on it. "All right," she said. "I accept your terms."

Ezra smirked. "I knew you'd see reason."

"I have one condition. You are not be anywhere near this house as Mr. Sloan conducts his investigation and interviews." When Ezra opened his mouth to protest, Ivy held up a finger to silence him. "Otherwise, I will fight you tooth and nail in court, and spend what my husband bequeathed to me in the process. If I'm guilty, this Mr.

Sloan will find out sooner rather than later." She raised an eyebrow at Mr. Sloan. "If you're one of the finest detectives in England it shouldn't be terribly difficult to prove my alleged misdeeds." She regretted her words almost as soon as she said them. The man's aura glowed in an extraordinary, unrecognizable way. He wasn't fully human. He would have ways of circumventing human ways of investigation, and she didn't know what they were, couldn't mount a defense.

Gods and goddesses above and below, she was fucked.

Ezra glared at her, his hatred and distrust palpable. Ivy ignored it and focused on the other man who didn't despise her. "Let me show you to my sitting room," she said. "We'll speak there." To Mr. Sloan, she added, "It will be two years this December since Edwin's passing."

MERRITT HOPED he kept his face schooled in a neutral expression throughout his encounter with Mrs. Thaddeus. He'd prided himself on his ability to do so when he still investigated murders and robberies on behalf of the Liverpool constabulary, but he'd never spoken to a suspect who rattled him the way she did.

For one thing, she was much younger than he expected, perhaps in her mid-thirties. Certainly young enough to be the late Dr. Thaddeus's daughter or Ezra's older sister. She was also beautiful: her half-mourning day dress was perfectly cut, revealing her hourglass figure that he suspected wasn't the product of stays and a bustle. Chestnut-colored hair pinned at the nape of her neck shone in the sunlight streaming through the sitting room windows. Her green eyes sparkled with curiosity, but there was an underlying wariness, not that it would be unexpected. She was a murder suspect, after all.

A white-aproned woman with iron gray hair brought tea on a silver service to them in the sitting room. Merritt and Ezra took seats opposite Mrs. Thaddeus, who sat on a small divan, taking care to arrange her skirts around her. Once the maid poured the tea, Mrs. Thaddeus said quietly, "That will be all, Martha. Thank you." She waited until Martha left before speaking again. "I fear you're wasting your time and funds," she said to Ezra, tone frosty. She turned to Merritt and pinned him with a hard stare. "My late husband died of natural causes. I'm happy to produce physicians' reports, as I've already told you. My stepson continues to insist that I murdered him for his estate."

Merritt matched her hard look, returning it with one of his own. He wasn't intimidated by her. While his own powers were fairly limited thanks to his human side, he did have his own magic. He would have to use it carefully to mount a defense against a witch. "Did you?" he asked.

Her color rose. "Of course I didn't."

"Note that she isn't insisting that she could never do such a thing because she loved him," Ezra snapped.

"You're investigating whether I murdered my husband, not my feelings for him," Mrs. Thaddeus returned smoothly. To Merritt, she said, "I did not kill my husband. How should I prove it to you?"

All Merritt had to do was summon the dead man's spirit and ask him directly. "You said you have physicians' reports?"

"Yes."

"May I look around the house, as well?"

Mrs. Thaddeus again pinned him with a stare, and he wondered what she was thinking. Had she recognized what he was? Likely not; fae descendants were incredibly rare. Like his vampire friends, all Mrs. Thaddeus could recognize was something off about him. An uncanny resemblance to a full human. He was damned if he could figure out what made him stand out to other supernatural creatures.

Something in Mrs. Thaddeus's countenance relaxed. "Yes. Look wherever you please. I have nothing to hide."

That almost certainly meant she had something to hide. Despite the gravity of the situation, Merritt couldn't help but be intrigued. He stood up. "I'd like to do that, then."

She tilted her head to the side, surprised. "Now?"

"Is there a better time that would work for you?"

She gave a pointed glance at Ezra, who smirked in response. "I suppose not." She sighed and rose to her feet. "I suppose the tea was a waste."

"It's from my funds, so I don't see why you're complaining." Ezra leaned back in his chair and took a dramatic sip from his cup that would've been out of place in any formal dining room.

Merritt may have come from a working-class family, but he loathed bad manners. He barely suppressed a shudder at the sound of slurping. Surely, he was doing it only to irritate Mrs. Thaddeus. He also stood and motioned to follow Mrs. Thaddeus. His notebook and pencil at the ready, he said, "After you."

A CURIOUS COMBINATION of anger and intrigue filled Ivy as she led the private detective through the house to her late husband's study. It was the only room she could think of to take Mr. Sloan to, the place where Edwin's records and formulas were kept, where she'd stored his autopsy reports.

Not that there was much to his formulas other than distilled water and a healthy dose of beet sugar, mixed with some herbs. Ivy had been the one to ensure its efficacy with her magic.

She and Edwin hadn't been in love, but they had respected each other. In that moment, she missed him fiercely. He'd been the closest thing she'd ever had to a best friend.

She forced all thoughts of Edwin out of her mind when she opened the study door and gestured for Mr. Sloan to walk in. "Take a look around." She pointed to the bookshelves built into the far wall. "His ledgers are there, as are his formulas for the Miracle Elixir over the years. I've left the autopsy reports on the desk."

Mr. Sloan picked up a leather-bound journal and rifled through it. "I take it you're not concerned about the elixir's formula falling into the wrong hands?"

She shrugged. "It's water, sugar, and dashes of valerian root and peppermint. Hardly a trade secret."

"Only valerian root?"

"Edwin ordered the removal of the laudanum years ago, before we met."

"An ethical patent medicine seller," Mr. Sloan mused. "I never would've considered that possible."

Ivy couldn't help but let her indignation show at that comment. "Edwin was an honorable man. I cannot say the same of his son."

"Yet without the laudanum, his Miracle Elixir is one of the most widely sold patent medicines in England, despite its ingredients being nothing more than beet sugar and water. It's renowned for its pain relief properties. Why is that?"

It was entirely due to Ivy's magic, but she could hardly reveal that. "The Miracle Elixir provides peace of mind.

Never underestimate the effect of peace of mind at a reasonable price."

That earned a smile from the detective. "I'll be certain not to."

Ivy had the impression that Mr. Sloan seldom smiled. It was a shame. His was nice to look at. She pushed aside that observation, remembering why he was here. The man wasn't fully human and he was investigating her for murder. She shouldn't go about admiring a man's smile when she didn't know what foe she was facing.

"May I take the autopsy reports?" he asked, inclining his head toward the desk.

"Of course. Feel free to contact the doctors who wrote them, too."

He crossed the room's distance to the desk and helped himself to the stack of papers there, tucking them under his arm. "Did you do it?" he asked noncommittally.

Surprise, then fury rose in her at the question. "No."

"You loved your husband?"

She nearly blurted yes, then stopped herself in time. She and Edwin had cared for each other, but theirs hadn't been a love story. Edwin's first wife, Ezra's mother Patricia, held the key to his heart years after she passed from consumption. Ivy doubted Mr. Sloan would believe her if she told him that she adored Edwin, anyway. "We were very close," she said.

"Was it a marriage of convenience?"

She flinched at the question. "If I say no, will you believe me?"

"No."

"Why not?"

"Younger women marrying men old enough to be their fathers is either the result of a vile arrangement between the groom and the bride's father's best friend, or the couple each having something the other wants."

"I was twenty-seven when I married Edwin," Ivy replied evenly. "I was hardly a child."

"How long were you married?"

"Nine years."

"Was it your first marriage?"

She didn't try to conceal her irritation at the question. "Yes."

"How did you manage to stay unmarried so long?"

Witches like her, who could earn a living with their gifts, seldom married. What was the point? She had more tools in her arsenal than the average man did to get herself ahead in life. "I preferred it," she replied.

"How did you and Dr. Thaddeus meet? Was he truly a physician?"

"He was, although he gave up his practice when he developed his Miracle Elixir."

"I imagine the patent medicine business is far more lucrative than seeing patients."

That comment irked her, too, but she nodded. Edwin had cared for people. It was one of the reasons he invented his medicine. He could help more people with it than physicking to individuals. It was why he sought her out, a respectable middle class self-made woman who had built a quiet underground business around her potions and creams, powered by her healing spells.

"Who has control of the elixir now?" Mr. Sloan asked.

"I do. He left the company to me."

"What about Ezra?"

"He's been set up with an enormous settlement and the family townhouses in Liverpool and London. Edwin didn't think he had the experience necessary to run the company.

Between the inheritances left to him from both his parents, he's better off financially than I'll ever be."

"And you do?"

She nodded again. For some strange reason, nervousness crested over her in a wave and her palms grew sweaty at the gravely notes in his voice. There was an intensity to him that touched something in her, a pull of otherworldly energy that she hadn't felt in, well, *ever*. If she didn't know any better, she might have suspected Mr. Sloan was part incubus. She shook her head a little, as if to physically dislodge the notion from her head. If the detective was an incubus, she would have torn off her clothes and thrown herself at him already.

He noticed. "Is something wrong?"

She didn't try to hide the sarcasm in her voice. "Other than being questioned again for a murder I didn't commit? My husband died of natural causes. It isn't unheard of in men his age." She glanced at a bust of a philosopher's head that rested on one of the bookshelves, a reproduction from an ancient world sculpture. For half a second, she wished to pick it up and hurl it across the study at his handsome face. She took a deep breath, trying to center herself and regaining her sense of decorum. "My apologies," she murmured. "Ezra has been harboring delusions about Edwin's death since he died."

"Were they close?"

Ivy hesitated, unsure how to answer. She chose her words carefully. "They were, once. They drifted apart as Ezra grew up. They didn't see eye to eye on many things and as I'm sure you've gathered, Ezra disapproved of our marriage."

Mr. Sloan nodded, then inclined his head at the desk. "May I look at your husband's effects?"

If it would get the detective out of her house, she

would agree to almost anything. She felt herself blush at the thought of what those things could be. "Yes," she replied. She was still in half-mourning. While she hadn't been in love with the man she wore the mourning clothes for, she still respected him and his memory. Her body taking notice of the private detective her stepson hired to prove her a killer was inappropriate, more so when she wasn't even sure what he was.

Mr. Sloan glanced over the desk, still arranged the way Edwin liked it. He picked up a few objects—his pens, his sealed inkwell, a small stone Ezra painted when he was a boy—and held them for a few seconds, as if meditating over them. Ivy watched, fascinated.

Was he a magic practitioner like she was? Likely not. She would have sensed his power as soon as he walked through the door. He didn't bear the smell of the outdoors that shifters so often had, nor could he be a vampire if he walked in the sunlight. A dhampir, perhaps? If such beings actually existed, she wouldn't be surprised to hear he was one of them. She waited, saying nothing, and pretended to look at the medical books on the shelves. Out of the corner of her eye, she saw Mr. Sloan quickly slip Edwin's favorite pen in his trouser pocket. She could hardly keep a smile off her face. He'd just ensured that she could find out who and what he really was.

"That will be all for today," Mr. Sloan announced.

"I'll see you out." Ivy held open the study door for him until he left the room, then closed it behind them on whisper-quiet hinges.

# CHAPTER 3

IT FELT like the pen Merritt stole was burning a hole in his pocket. He ignored the sensation. The pen had been nearly hot to the touch when he picked it up. It was a symbol of the fondness the late Dr. Thaddeus had for it, a talisman that represented his soul. As his ornithopter took off to the gray sky above, he idly wondered why the dead man cared for it so much. It was a poor attempt to keep his thoughts away from his widow.

Mrs. Thaddeus absolutely despised him, that much was certain. The knowledge was rankling, which was unusual. Merritt usually didn't care what others thought of him. Even so, he couldn't help but look forward to the next time he had to see her.

Would there be a next time after he summoned Dr. Thaddeus's spirit? If the man truly had died of natural causes, there was no need to call on his widow again.

As he sailed over the countryside, he went over his impressions of the house. There was a dark energy there but it was unrelated to Mrs. Thaddeus. He believed her when she insisted she hadn't killed her husband. Whether he had actually died of a heart ailment, Merritt couldn't say until he spoke to his ghost.

He couldn't let himself relax until he had returned to Liverpool and stowed his ornithopter on the roof of the four-story building he called home. He unlocked the roof's exterior door and let himself into the building, descending the stairs until he reached his second floor flat. He let himself in, locking the door behind him, then removed the pilfered pen from his pocket.

It was a gaudy thing, a brass implement engraved with the late doctor's initials in a looping, cursive hand. A tarnished silver caduceus was affixed to the end. Edwin Thaddeus had used this pen to write down innumerable formulas for his patent medicine, written countless prescriptions for laudanum and willow bark before he left his practice. He'd felt the attachment the dead man had to it before he touched it. Even now, in the waning early evening light flowing through his window, he could see it glowing under his necromancer's eye.

Dr. Thaddeus had loved this pen.

Merritt left it on the altar he used to summon spirits at home and fixed himself a drink. As soon as the first drops of whiskey hit his glass, a throat cleared behind him. He closed his eyes and sighed before saying, "You're early." He turned around to face Claudia, his building's resident ghost and his occasional roommate.

Her form glowed, her brown wool stola nearly blending in with the flat's drab furnishings. While Claudia's body form was transparent and without substance, her features were still distinct. In life, Merritt knew her hair would have shone glossy black in the sunlight and her dark eyes sparkled. "I wasn't expecting you to return so soon," Claudia replied. "It's a pleasant surprise."

"Don't you have anywhere else to haunt?"

"Yes, but it's very boring after you've done it for a thousand years. I thought you were spending time in Londonium."

He didn't bother correcting her. Claudia wouldn't refer to London by its current name, ever, so there wasn't any point. "I was only there a few days," Merritt replied. "Some of my friends have recently returned from a trip abroad and I wanted to catch up with them before they leave again. It also turns out the new case I've been hired for can be investigated closer to home." He took a healthy swallow of his whiskey. "So, here I am."

"It's nice to have company again." Claudia primly sat down on the brown and gray stuffed settee against the wall. How she did that when she had no solid form, Merritt didn't know. "How are your friends? Was this the vampire couple?"

Merritt nodded. "Watching them paw each other can get rather disgusting."

"You'll have to have them visit you sometime. I don't think I've ever met a vampire."

"What makes you so sure they could see you?" Merritt countered.

"*You* can."

"I'm a necromancer. It comes with the territory."

"It stands to reason a vampire would be able to see me. We're different kinds of dead. We would have a lot in common."

Merritt knew his resident ghost would wax eternal about her loneliness if he didn't change the subject, so he did. "I have someone to summon," he said, inclining his head at the altar.

That got Claudia's attention. "Who?"

"It's for the case I've been hired to do. His son hired me to find out if his stepmother killed his father."

Claudia leaned forward, a conspiratorial smile on her lips. "Did she do it?"

"I don't think she did." The words left Merritt's mouth before he could think them over. "It's just a hunch I have."

"Your hunches usually prove correct."

"I've been wrong before." Merritt pinched the bridge of his nose between his fingers, dreading the barrage of questions Claudia would throw at him with his next statement. "His widow is a witch."

Claudia clapped her hands together in delight. "I haven't spoken to a witch since the last time my fortune was read!"

That had to be a millennia ago. "I can't say I've ever dealt with one. This isn't someone who sells her potions to a gullible crowd. I sensed real power coming off her."

"That doesn't mean she's using her power for evil," Claudia pointed out. "You're a descendant of the unseelie fae and you've managed to keep yourself from stealing a baby."

"Why the hell would I steal a baby?"

She looked at him like he was an idiot. "For changelings."

Merritt sighed. Speaking to Claudia sometimes felt like he was speaking to a precocious child, even though she had to have been in her twenties when she died. She'd been wandering the site where his flat was for centuries, since Britain was a Roman settlement, and Merritt suspected she had gone a little mad from the lack of socialization through the years. She'd told him the first time she appeared that he was the fourth person she'd spoken to since she died. "I have no use for changelings," he said. "If any fae still exist, I doubt they'd bother with changelings anymore."

"But the power is still there. Deep down, there must be

a desire to wreak destruction. You've managed to avoid doing so."

"The human side won out. I use my abilities for good." He nodded again at the altar. "I'm going to summon that pen owner's ghost, ask him how he died, and collect the five hundred pounds his son offered."

"Then you'll return his property to his widow," Claudia added helpfully.

He supposed he would. "I'll get to see her again." He didn't know he'd spoken the words aloud until he saw Claudia's grinning face.

"Is she a pretty widow?"

What was the point in lying? Claudia couldn't tell anyone he was attracted to a murder suspect. "Yes."

"Witches were always beautiful in my time, too."

Mrs. Thaddeus wasn't just beautiful, she was striking. There was a quiet, self-assured elegance to her that would have every head turning when she walked into a room. Merritt liked a confident woman who could command attention with a single glance. "I suppose it's moot, since it would be terribly unprofessional of me to chase after a widow, still in mourning, accused of murder."

Claudia smoothed her stola's skirt and adjusted her tunic's cuffs, habits she'd had as long as Merritt had known her. When she sat, her clothes were little more than blurs of color. "You only live once."

"Unless you're a vampire or ghost."

She shrugged. "I chose to stay on this plane after my death. If I wanted to leave, I could. Or I could just ask you to exorcise me."

Merritt couldn't keep himself from shuddering at the word. "I'd rather not do that."

She rose and glided to the altar. Not having substantial

form, she couldn't pick up the pen, but she peered at it all the same. "Do you need my help?"

"I'll be fine, although you're welcome to stay, if you'd like to speak to him. Spirit to spirit."

"I'm a *ghost*," she said indignantly.

Merritt didn't distinguish between the two, but he wasn't about to pick a fight with the actual ghost who sometimes shared his flat. He lit a black candle on the altar and concentrated, holding the pen in his hand, eyes closed in concentration. "*Spiritus, praecipio tibi it resurgas de loco tuo in caelis*," he murmured, the only Latin phrase he knew.

"You mispronounced 'praecipio,'" Claudia chirped.

A strange energy traveled up his arm and he dropped the pen on the altar. The energy ceased. Confused, Merritt opened his eyes. Claudia's form floated next to the altar. "Did you do that?" he asked sharply.

"Do what?"

"Frighten him off."

"Of course not. I can't believe you'd think I would do such a thing," she huffed. "I don't think your spirit wants to be summoned. Or maybe something's keeping him from being summoned."

A chill threaded through Merritt. When he looked at the pen, he saw the glow was gone. It was an ordinary pen again, well-used and tarnished. Whatever hold the late Dr. Thaddeus had to it, it was gone. "Son of a bitch," he hissed.

"I think your spirit might have actually been murdered by his witch wife," Claudia interpreted, ever helpful.

"Fuck me." Merritt needed another drink.

"No, thank you. I can't, anyway."

Merritt sidestepped that remark and picked up the whiskey bottle still sitting on the kitchen table. He poured another drink and tossed it back. "Ezra Thaddeus is really going to make me earn those five hundred pounds."

~

Ivy HATED CITIES. London was the worst, with Liverpool being a close second. The smells were unbearable, there were too many people, and she had to expend more energy than she wanted ensuring she wasn't about to be pickpocketed.

The only redeeming quality about tonight's jaunt was that Liverpool was fairly close to her home and Merritt Sloan seemed to live in a respectable neighborhood. It was older, the houses at least half a century old, but they appeared to be well-maintained. Every now and then an ornithopter lurched about overhead as it jostled for space on a roof, or a dirigible sailed above. There must be an airfield nearby.

The spell Ivy cast to find Edwin's pen stayed effective as she trod the streets, looking for the house where the pen was. It was odd: she felt normal again in Liverpool, that her magic had finally fully returned. If she stayed longer in the hotel room she'd rented for the night, she was certain she could cast anything and it would work. There was something wrong with her house, something there to dampen her abilities. Her elation at finding out where the detective had squirreled away her husband's favorite pen vanished as she realized what this meant. Someone, possibly Ezra or a friend of his, had cast something over the house to render her magic ineffective. How did Ezra know she was a witch in the first place?

Perhaps she should hire the detective for her own purposes, once she proved to him that she hadn't killed her husband.

The spell guided her down the street, and she felt the pull of the house where Merritt Sloan had to live as if he was physically dragging her there. She felt a blush touch her cheeks at the thought of his hands on her anywhere. She had to stop and collect herself for a few seconds. Taking a deep breath, she stared at the house. It was tall, thin, and stretched four floors into the sky. The pen was somewhere in there.

Anticipation coursed through her veins as she climbed the stairs to the front door. Locked, of course, but that was easily dealt with via a quick spell muttered under her breath. She stepped into a foyer lit with wall-mounted gas lamps, the light turned low. A list of tenant names rested on the wall above a line of bell pulls. According to it, M. Sloan lived on the second floor. Without bothering to ring it, she walked up another staircase, this one narrow enough so she could touch the walls on either side of her without stretching her arms. It felt close and claustrophobic, exactly the reason she hated cities. The locating spell indicated that the pen was in the flat whose door was to her right. Steeling herself, she knocked on it and waited. It opened, revealing Mr. Sloan in his shirtsleeves.

He stared at her in shock.

"Good evening," Ivy said primly. "I'm here for the pen you stole from my husband's study."

It took a few seconds for her words to register. He looked like he wanted to argue, but he stepped aside. "Please come in."

Was she about to be murdered? She had a knife concealed in her skirt pocket and protection spells at the ready, as long as she could cast them. She needed her hands and mouth free to do that. Edwin's pen was here. She didn't have much choice. She stepped into the flat.

It was small and cozy, albeit plain in its simple

furnishings. The room she stood in functioned as a lounge and kitchen. The kitchen's accessories were old steam and clock-powered things that had to be nearly as old as she was. There were two doors off the main room that she assumed led to the bedroom and a water closet. Her estimation of the building went up a little, if the flats had their own cooking and bathing spaces. She spotted the pen sitting on a small, high table, the wood scarred and worn smooth from age. A single, half-burned black candle rested next to it on a brass tray. Something in Ivy twisted as she realized what she was looking at: an altar. "Wizard," she breathed, before she could stop herself.

He was quiet for a moment. "Not exactly."

She silently chastised herself for expressing concern over his altar. She should've simply strode across the room, taken it back, and stomped out of his flat. "What the hell are you?"

"What are *you*?" he countered. "What kind of witch?"

Damn it, he knew what she was. She kept her lips pressed together for fear she would cast a spell to knock him clear across the room. She didn't want to do that until she knew what she was dealing with.

"Do you practice dark arts or do you make the crops grow?" he continued. There was a taunting note in his voice that she already hated.

She gave him what she hoped was her most haughty look. "A lady can do both."

"You're a witch, not a lady."

She narrowed her eyes at him. "I can be both." She grabbed the pen and put it in her skirt pocket, next to her knife.

He didn't try to stop her. "You may as well take it. I couldn't get anything from it. You've managed to banish his spirit from this plane into another dimension I can't possibly access."

Her stomach dropped. "You're a necromancer," Ivy deduced. She'd never met one before, but she'd heard of them. Descended from the extinct unseelie fae, capable of shapeshifting and raising the dead, thieves of children.

He held out his hands, as if to illustrate that it was obvious.

"Have you been drinking?" she asked.

"I've had a couple. I've never not been able to communicate with a spirit before and thought I deserved them."

She recalled his earlier remark about her banishing his spirit. "I did not kill my husband, and I didn't send his soul anywhere." Her words were clipped, even in her controlled anger. She hoped he didn't detect the note of fear in her voice. She didn't know what he was capable of.

Mr. Sloan looked like he wanted to say something, thought better of it, and closed his mouth.

"His heart failed." Ivy's ire rose, overtaking her fright. The frustration and helplessness she'd felt since Ezra started his ridiculous accusations caught up with her. She felt like screaming in his face until her voice was hoarse. Gods and goddesses damn it all, why couldn't everyone just leave her be? "He was sixty-seven years old," she continued, hating the catch in her voice. "It isn't uncommon for men of his age and dispositions to pass away unexpectedly. I miss him." An undignified sniffle escaped her. She had to get out of this flat before she made more of a scene than she'd already had. She was at the door when a proprietary hand was placed on her arm.

"Wait," Mr. Sloan said.

She shook him off. "No." Willing her tears away, she asked, "How much is my stepson paying you?"

His answer was immediate. "Five hundred pounds."

"I'll double it if you set this whole affair aside, tell Ezra that his father wasn't murdered, and leave me alone."

"I can't do that, madam."

"Why the hell not?" The epithet slipped out before she could stop herself.

"I've been hired to see this through all the way." He paused and tilted his head to the side, as if listening to someone who wasn't there.

Ivy was finished with the conversation and the idiot detective. "Don't bother me again," she ordered him before she walked out of the flat. She closed the door behind her. As she reached for the stairs' banister, she heard him speaking through the door.

"I will do no such thing."

She waited, listening, before he spoke again after a pause.

"In the morning. It's too late now and I'm in no state to be doing that."

Was he mad, dangerous, or a combination of both? Where the hell had Ezra found this detective? Gods and goddesses above and below, the man knew where she lived. Her magic wasn't working when she was there. As she descended the stairs, she considered running away, but knew that would only make her look guilty in the eyes of Ezra and the law. She was also still responsible for the patent medicine business. She stepped back on to the street, grateful to be outside again, and walked to her hotel, hoping Mr. Sloan didn't have his own way of tracking her down.

# CHAPTER 4

THREE DAYS PASSED before Merritt returned to the Thaddeus home. Ezra had sent him a cable that demanded his progress on the case thus far, and with reluctance Merritt boarded his ornithopter for another journey. He knew he hadn't accomplished anything that would justify what Ezra was paying him.

His inability to summon Edwin Thaddeus's spirit rankled him. He knew he hadn't lost it altogether, since he could still see and speak with Claudia. When he left his flat to shop for groceries, he spotted the spirits that lingered around the butcher shop and greengrocer's. It was simply Dr. Thaddeus that he couldn't reach, and he guessed he'd have to return to the house to try again.

It was late morning when he landed his ornithopter at the foot of the Thaddeus home grounds, unusually bright and warm for mid-October. Dread lodged itself in his gut as he walked up the cobblestone path. He'd made an absolute ass of himself the last time they spoke. The one time someone dropped by his flat to chat, he'd been well on his way to being drunk. Claudia's chattering at him about Mrs. Thaddeus while he tried to speak with the widow hadn't helped, either. The ghost saw so few people that anyone new would be a novelty.

He knocked on the door and waited. Martha the housekeeper opened it, her apron crisp and bright white. "Yes?" Her voice was all business, no-nonsense.

"I'm here to pay a call to Mrs. Thaddeus."

"She's unavailable."

Merritt waited to see if she would give a hint about her employer's return, but the woman's expression was blank. "May I leave something for her?" He withdrew a sealed envelope from his coat pocket. Inside was a brief apology note for his behavior the other night.

The housekeeper accepted it without another word and closed the door in his face. The iron and brass knocker clapped against the wood.

Merritt sighed. He looked around the grounds, at the well-maintained shrubs and trees. The flower beds were covered in burlap to protect against the impending winter and he idly wondered what they would look like in full bloom.

Dr. Thaddeus was found dead in his garden. Perhaps something there could link Merritt to his spirit, a forgotten shovel or something. Not being a gardener, Merritt didn't know what to look for. He wandered around the house, following a pebbled path that meandered around the trees. On either side of him were more covered flower beds and shrubs he couldn't identify, and none of the pull he felt when a spirit was nearby. Instead, an unfamiliar thrum vibrated through him, otherworldly and insistent as a drumbeat.

Witch magic, perhaps?

Something slammed into him from above and he fell into an empty flowerbed with an undignified curse. "Fuck!" He was flat on his back, the triumphant face of Mrs. Thaddeus above him.

She had him pinned down on the ground, her lower half a swirl of lavender and gray skirts.

"What is the meaning of this?" he asked. When he tried to lift his hands, her grip strengthened. He could shove her off, but for some bizarre reason he found he didn't want to just yet.

"I could ask the same thing of you. Why are you wandering around my home like it's a public museum?" she retorted.

"Technically, it was the garden. What are you doing, sitting in trees?"

Her reply was firm. "Technically, it's part of my home. Answer my question."

"I came to apologize. I'd also like to know why you jumped on me."

Her mouth opened in a round O of surprise and she let go of his wrists.

Merritt remained where he was, not wanting to startle her further. His coat would be a mess of dirt when he finally rose.

"I see." She leaned back and swung one of her legs away from his body where she'd been straddling him, then rolled over to sit on the ground next to him. "I saw you walking up my drive again and knew you would come looking for me. I wanted to catch you in the act, which I suppose I did. I also owe you an apology as well. No one wants an uninvited guest." A wry smile crossed her lips. "No one wants to be pounced on, either."

Merritt wasn't so sure about that last part, although he

would've preferred it in other circumstances. He hauled himself up to better face her. "I stole your husband's property and was drunk when you arrived to take it back," Merritt pointed out. The reasons for how she could do that were at his mind's forefront, and he wanted those details. "How did you do it?"

"You've already guessed I'm a witch. I cast a seeking spell." She turned her head to face him. "Who were you talking to in your flat?"

"Would you think me a madman if I said it's the ghost who haunts the flat across the corridor from mine?"

"No, I suppose not." She stood up and Merritt followed suit. "You said you're a necromancer. Is that why you were trying to summon my husband?"

He nodded. "I couldn't."

"Is that a common problem?"

"Not for me." He hated having to explain this next part. He couldn't *believe* he was going to explain this next part. "I've never not been able to summon a spirit since I came into my ability." He cleared his throat. "I believe he may have been murdered, after all." As her expression shifted to one of outrage, he added, "I no longer believe you did it."

She tilted her head, full lips set in a tense line. "How?"

"For one, you have no necromancer abilities. Only a necromancer could banish someone to the ether or trap him, which is what I believe happened to your husband's soul."

"Edwin is trapped in some kind of purgatory?" Her angry expression gave way to one of grief. She looked like she might cry.

"I don't know. But he isn't in the afterlife that we can reach. I believe he was murdered and someone with supernatural abilities committed it." He'd mulled over that possibility during his flight to the countryside. He stood up and held out his hand for her. She looked at it in surprise before taking it and allowing him to haul her to her feet.

The color had drained from her face. "You really believe he was murdered," she said softly.

"I believe someone wanted him out of the way. Why, I couldn't tell you yet. If I could summon him, I could ask him directly."

"Is that how you usually conduct your investigations?"

"When someone has turned up dead, yes. In matters of stolen property, missing persons, and the like, I have other methods." Thanks to his fae side. At least he'd inherited all of the useful fae bits.

She sighed, an angry sound. "I suppose we should sit down inside and discuss this like adults." She inclined her head toward the house. "Come with me."

Ivy couldn't believe she was doing this. She led Mr. Sloan through the garden paths to the kitchen door, holding it open for him. He doffed his hat and rubbed the spot where his neck met his shoulder. Guilt twanged through her at the sight. She opened a cabinet and removed a small bottle, holding it out to him. "For the pain," she said.

He turned it over in his hands, peering at the hand-written label. "What is this?"

"A ginger poultice for muscle pain. I made it myself."

"Enchanted or not?"

"Not, nor is it poisoned."

"I should tell you that when a detective hears the words

'it's not poison,' he'll automatically assume that it *is* poison." Despite the gravity of his words, Mr. Sloan had a small smile on his lips.

"I have no reason to poison you. Although we have much to discuss, speaking of poisoning and other methods of murder."

Just as quickly, Mr. Sloan's smile dropped.

For some strange reason, she hated to be the cause of it. She suspected he didn't smile often. It was a shame; he had a nice one. She led Mr. Sloan through the house, passing Martha, her housekeeper on the way. "Bring us some tea and biscuits to my study."

Martha nodded.

Trepidation coursed through her as she walked through the house, up a flight of stairs to the locked room she used as a study. The only other person who ever ventured into it was her late husband, who liked to watch her cast spells. Ivy used to keep the room locked with one. Since Edwin died and her magic faded, she'd had to resort to using a heavy brass lock and key. She hoped she wasn't about to make a mistake, allowing Mr. Sloan inside. She threw back the window's drapes, letting in weak autumn sunshine to stream over her myriad books and jars. Pots of herbs were crammed in a set of bookshelves against the opposite wall, while others were laid out to dry on a table. Her mortar and pestle waited for her on a scarred wooden desk.

"Is this where the magic happens?" Mr. Sloan asked as he took in the room.

"I suppose so." A small closet was hidden behind the bookcase, but she didn't reveal it. That was where she kept her grimoires and other magical implements, passed down in her family.

A witch had to keep some secrets.

She didn't speak until Martha left a tray of tea and biscuits on her desk. Ivy closed the door behind her, hating what she had to admit next. "It stands to reason that something supernatural was behind Edwin's death." Steeling her nerves, she continued, "My magic has dried up in the months since he died, at least when I'm at home. It returned when I went looking for you the other night."

"Oh?" Mr. Sloan patted his pockets, then removed his notebook and pencil.

Ivy stared at it, agog. "You're going to write this down?"

"Why not? It's extremely pertinent to the case."

"What if someone finds it? I don't want the general public to know that the secret behind Dr. Thaddeus's Miracle Elixir is magic. Witches haven't exactly been welcomed into English society with open arms."

"I beg to differ. Have you missed the spiritualism movement?"

"That's for séances," Ivy replied. "Which begs the question why you aren't hosting séances for far more money than you could earn as a private detective."

"I'd prefer not to attract more attention to myself from the dead than I already do. Once they know you're willing to talk to them, they never leave you alone. Ghosts can get lonely."

Curiosity had her sidestepping the issue at hand. "Like the one in your flat?"

"Claudia officially haunts the flat across the corridor from mine and is the reason tenants never stay longer than a month or two. She's gone a little mad over the centuries," Mr. Sloan said. There was a touch of sadness in his voice. "She's never told me why she insists on staying on the mortal plane."

"How long?"

"Since London was Londinium. She's never told me how she came about to be haunting a flat in Liverpool and I don't push." Mr. Sloan inclined his head toward her table where herbs were spread out to dry. "You said you lost your magic."

Ivy pushed out the thought of the lonely, mad ghost wandering the earth for over a millennia and back to her own dilemma. "I started losing my magic shortly after Edwin died. I thought it was related to grief, both from his passing and Ezra's accusations. It's been steadily decreasing since then, and since I entered half-mourning, it's been nearly stagnant. My protection and warding spells won't last while I'm at home. My sensing spells don't have the range they used to. Everything is restored after I'm away from the property."

"What about the elixir?"

"The spell I use on the elixir is very simple and has always been successfully cast when I visit the factory." Now that Ivy was talking about it, she felt like a world-class idiot for not having noticed the connection earlier. Grief and harassment had a way of messing with the logical parts of one's thought processes.

"Perhaps you could better help me investigate your husband's death if you left the house," Mr. Sloan said.

Ivy blinked in surprise at his suggestion. "I was under the impression that you were employed by my stepson."

"I am, but our contract doesn't have any stipulations about who I can and cannot ask for help. He hired me because I have a preternatural knack for solving mysteries." A thoughtful look crossed his face. "Does Ezra know you're a witch?"

Ivy shook her head. "It was kept strictly between Edwin and I. No one else knows what I am, except for you, my sister and her family."

"Where's your sister now?"

"Happily living in Dundee. Her husband is descended from witches, too. My nieces and nephews inherited Isabel's abilities."

"If your husband utilized magical abilities for his products, it stands to reason that other people in his circle could have, as well. That would explain why your magic doesn't work here."

"I would have felt it if the property was hexed."

"I would have, too," Mr. Sloan said.

She hadn't expected that. "Could necromancers sense such a thing?"

The detective actually flushed at the question. He looked away, as if he'd accidentally let something slip.

"Mr. Sloan," she said, putting as much firmness into her voice as she could. "Is there something else you're not telling me? Can you cast spells?"

"Not exactly."

"What is it you're keeping from me?"

He picked up a biscuit, ate it, and didn't answer.

Ivy gritted her teeth and sipped her tea, waiting for him to collect himself.

"I'm part fae. Probably half fae with how much is in my background," he finally mumbled.

That wasn't what she'd been expecting. "I beg your pardon?"

"Each of my parents is part fae," he repeated. "Descended from the unseelie court, I'm afraid, not that it exists now."

Ivy nodded. Fae had loved humans, both for themselves and for torturing them, so much that they bred themselves out of existence. "Where does the necromancer part of you fit into this?"

"Necromancy comes from the unseelie fae."

So, he was a half fae necromancer, with roots in dark magic. "Can you raise the dead?"

He hesitated. A shadow crossed over his face. "I prefer to communicate with spirits."

"You're more of a medium, then."

"No, mediums aren't real." He smiled. "As you pointed out, I suppose I could set up a profitable fraud by holding false séances, but ghosts tend to seek me out. If I deliberately called on them and ignored whoever responded, they would never leave me be, ever. Ghosts rarely wander the earth if they're happy with their lot in the afterlife."

Ivy leaned forward, eager to hear more about the other side. "Can you see heaven or hell?"

"No. What happens after death is still largely a mystery, even to me."

Ivy had hoped that Edwin was happy after he died, wherever he was, that he'd been reunited with his first wife. His being trapped in some horrible form of purgatory without her was a horrifying prospect. "How shall I help you speak to my husband?"

"Do you know any other magic practitioners? Can you research spells that would account for someone being unable to communicate with a necromancer?"

"Only my sister. I can wire her immediately. I'll also check my grimoires for black magic spells that count account for something like this."

"What would you say to your sister?"

"We can communicate in code. As I told you, she's discreet."

Mr. Sloan nodded. "Very good."

Tapping at the door interrupted him. "Mr. Thaddeus is here, madam." Martha's tone was weary. She was just as tired of this ordeal as Ivy was.

Ivy's heart sank. She sighed. "Thank you, Martha." To Mr. Sloan, she said, "I'm sure he'll want to speak to you, too."

He looked irritated at the prospect. "Of course, he will."

# CHAPTER 5

Ezra Thaddeus's arms were crossed over his chest, mouth pursed in irritation, a picture of frustration while he waited in Mrs. Thaddeus's sitting room. While Merritt no longer shared the view that Mrs. Thaddeus had murdered her husband, he understood how his client felt: stymied and powerless. "I spotted your ornithopter at the foot of the drive," Ezra announced by way of greeting, ignoring Mrs. Thaddeus.

The rude gesture, small as it was, rankled Merritt on the lady's behalf. "I had a few things to investigate here," Merritt replied.

"It's your job, is it not? Is this not what I'm paying you five hundred pounds for?"

Even Merritt, a working-class lad from the Liverpool tenements knew it was impolite to discuss money. He tamped down his irritation. "Investigations of this type often require a number of visits," he said stiffly. "I could hardly see the breadth of this house in one visit, could I?"

Something shifted in Ezra's demeanor. "You've found

evidence of murder?" He gave a pointed look at Mrs. Thaddeus.

Merritt silently cursed himself for not having considered what he would say to his client about Dr. Thaddeus's death. He kept his voice even and cool, "I have reasonable grounds to suspect that his death wasn't entirely natural. But if it wasn't, it was not at the hands or machinations of your stepmother."

A shadow crossed over Ezra's face. "Who the hell else could it have been?"

"Who the hell also had something to gain from your father's death?" The epithet slipped out before Merritt could stop himself. "I have yet to see Dr. Thaddeus's last will and find out who his other beneficiaries are."

"The business and this house were left to Ivy."

"What about you?" Merritt pressed.

"Some properties, my mother's belongings, and a trust." Ezra's voice was just as controlled as Merritt's. The thought struck him that if they were boys on a street, they would already be brawling. It was the presence of Mrs. Thaddeus that kept them civil, for different reasons. Ezra didn't want to give up the illusion of control, and Merritt...

He thought for a second. Merritt didn't want to make an ass out of himself in front of her. For some weird reason, it was vitally important that she respected him. It was just because he saw so few people with supernatural abilities. It had to be. Not because of her strength, the way she held herself, or the weight of her pressed against him when she dropped out of that tree, as brief as it was.

"Mr. Sloan."

Mrs. Thaddeus's voice pulled him out of his ruminations. He had the distinct impression he'd missed out on hearing something vital. "I beg your pardon?"

"Woolgathering during a murder investigation. Unbelievable," Ezra muttered.

"I'd like to remind you that you sought me out because of my success rate in solving cases. You didn't tell me who the other beneficiaries were, if there were any."

"There was a significant bequeath to someone else," Mrs. Thaddeus said. "While I own the business, the day-to-day operations have been left to Edwin's business partner, Roger McCann. He received a cash settlement and has rights to fifty percent of the net profits."

Merritt didn't have much of a head for large business, but even to him, half of the profits and no ownership seemed stingy to a partner. "I see."

Ezra narrowed his eyes at him. "Why the devil haven't you looked at the will yet or asked about it?"

Merritt could have kicked himself for not having done so sooner. His preferred *modus operandi* was to summon spirits and find out answers that way. Between Dr. Thaddeus's spirit being blocked from the mortal plane and the distraction his widow was proving to be, Merritt had been a piss-poor private detective on this case thus far. God damn it all, he was actually going to have to roll up his sleeves and investigate something the old-fashioned way. "I was investigating other aspects of this case first," he replied stiffly. "If I may be frank, in most cases in which a wealthy person has died suspiciously, it's usually their spouse who has done it."

Mrs. Thaddeus's dark brows rose and her full lips turned down in outrage.

He tried not to cringe. He would have to apologize to her later.

"But you said that you don't believe Ivy killed Father," Ezra said.

"No."

Mrs. Thaddeus visibly relaxed.

"How did you come to this conclusion?"

"I haven't come to any yet. Call it a hunch." Merritt was stalling. How should he explain to his client that he worked with gut instincts borne of magic? He'd never bungled a case like this before, let alone so early in the investigation.

"I'm disappointed. Your references said you could solve a case in half the time as other detectives and a quarter of the time as the Liverpool police." Ezra crossed his arms over his chest, waiting for a further explanation.

Merritt had none. "I'll be reading the will and taking a tour of the business shortly." Perhaps he could pick up something at the elixir's bottling plant, a spectral trace of Dr. Thaddeus's last days. He had observed such phenomena before.

"You need to tour the factory to solve the case?" Ezra asked. There was more than a touch of disdain and disbelief in his voice.

"My methods aren't entirely orthodox, which is why they produce the results they do," Merritt replied, tone curt. "You hired me to find out what happened to your father. I will do that. I also feel comfortable telling you that I don't believe Mrs. Thaddeus had anything to do with his death."

Ezra stared at him, aghast, then turned his gaze to Mrs. Thaddeus. "You're unbelievable," he muttered. Merritt wasn't sure if he was referring to himself or his stepmother. To Merritt, he said, "I want another update within a week. A proper one."

"You shall have it." Merritt desperately hoped that he would be able to make contact with the dead doctor by then, or have something that would exonerate his widow other than his gut instinct.

"I will consider our contract terminated if I don't have a satisfactory answer by then," Ezra added.

Merritt nodded. "Understood."

It wasn't until Ezra strode out of the house than Mrs. Thaddeus spoke. "Bastard," she hissed.

"Which of us are you referring to?"

She gave Merritt a look that clearly questioned his intelligence. He couldn't help but smile at it. A sparkle appeared in her eye for a brief moment. Just as quickly, it was gone, replaced by desolation. "Are you certain that you can find out what happened to my husband by Ezra's deadline?" she asked.

He wanted to see that look on her face again and hated that he would have to answer the way he did. "No."

She looked away for a moment, considering her words. When she spoke, her voice was low, conspiratorial. "Could you raise my husband from the dead?"

A wave of surprise, then revulsion flowed through Merritt. "Not after a year and a half." He'd seen plenty of dead bodies in his time. Before he knew what powers he held, he'd accidentally raised a few unfortunate animals back from the dead when he was young. The memory of the poor rabbit his childhood dog slaughtered rose to mind but even the memory of the dead rabbit was no match for the one of his grandfather, lying in bed, so still…

He closed his eyes for a few seconds, willing away the image.

He must have given away his discomfort at the notion because Mrs. Thaddeus quickly said, "Never mind. It's a horrific idea."

"You've been accused of murder. Someone desperate to prove their innocence will grasp at anything to do so, Mrs. Thaddeus. Unfortunately, I cannot raise your husband from the head."

She pinched the bridge of her nose in frustration. "Just call me Ivy."

"That's a bit familiar." Even as he said the words, Merritt regretted them. A part of him was delighted that she wanted him to do so, although he was damned if he could figure out why.

"I suppose if you're going to defend me against the very person who is paying you to prove I killed my husband, you should have the right to call me by my name." She sighed and rolled her shoulders. "There must be a way that I can help."

"You can start by showing me your husband's will and escorting me to the factory."

"I'll have the carriage readied." Mrs. Thaddeus—Ivy, he corrected himself—started to walk to the sitting room doorway, but Merritt placed a hand on her forearm, halting her.

She looked at him, awestruck for a second.

"Are you averse to flying there?" he asked.

As was the case with most other witches, save those with the blood of other supernatural species running in their veins, Ivy couldn't fly but she craved it. She welcomed it, and was only too happy to step into Mr. Sloan's ornithopter basket.

As the conveyance's wings flapped and it rose in the air, he asked her, "Can you do this on a broom?"

"Are you a mind reader in addition to a necromancer and unseelie fae, Mr. Sloan?"

"I hardly consider the fae part of me to count. And you may as well call me Merritt. My friends do."

A warm feeling spread through her at the invitation,

even though she'd insisted on his using her given name first. "Merritt, then. Are you a mind reader?" She leaned over the edge of the basket, taking in the sight of her house on the hilltop.

"No. It would make my job a lot easier if I was. Are you bothered by heights?" Steam issued from the ornithopter's vents and it bobbed a little higher in the air.

"No."

"The last woman in here nearly keeled over in the basket. She found out the hard way that she *loathes* heights. We weren't even that high up."

For some odd reason, jealousy flared in Ivy. She tore her gaze away from the ground to look at him. "Who?"

He kept his eyes on the navigation instruments ahead of him. He sounded distracted when he replied. "Oh, Elora Stone? One of my friends." He considered his words for a moment. "My mistake, I suppose she's Elora Lang now."

Relief welled in her. That probably meant his friend was married. Ivy tucked away that tiny bit of information for later, then felt a little off about it. She was still in half-mourning, after all. "The factory is close to Albert Dock," she said, changing the subject. "There's a public airfield nearby. We can walk from there."

He nodded. "I'm familiar with the area. A lot of bodies wash up on docks."

"And you commune with their spirits?"

"Yes. The newly dead are often confused, angry, or both. They're only too happy to tell me and anyone nearby who can listen about how they came to be stabbed to death or drowned." The ornithopter dipped. A thrill coursed through Ivy at the sensation, even though the logical part of her brain told her she should be alarmed at it.

"Can you release them?" Ivy asked.

"You mean, can I send them on their merry way to the afterlife? I can, but I don't. I always encourage them to leave on their own."

"What about the ghost in your flat?"

Merritt sighed. "Excellent question. I wish she was forthcoming about her reasons."

"Is she happy?"

"I can't tell. I think she's very lonely. She keeps driving out lodgers whenever they try to rent the flat across the corridor from mine. She's a very noisy ghost."

"She's never told you why she haunts the place?"

"Nothing specific other than she likes being on the mortal plane." A wistful note had crept into his voice. "I'd miss her if she left for the afterlife, but she's stayed behind for a reason. Perhaps she'll tell me someday, if she still remembers it."

Ivy couldn't imagine existing that long.

She didn't ask further about Claudia and instead let herself enjoy the ornithopter ride. The breeze pulled a few strands of hair out of the tidy knot at the base of her neck below her hat, and for a few moments she wished she could take out the style, let her hair be free. Of course, she wouldn't do that. She was already skirting the edge of propriety, being out and about while in half-mourning with a man at her side. Ivy missed wearing her hair loose, missed wearing colors.

Merritt expertly landed the ornithopter at the Albert Dock airfield, a process Ivy couldn't help but watch. His face was a mask of concentration and patience as a wind gust bucked the craft, making Ivy grab its edge for balance.

"Sorry," he said sheepishly.

Once it was anchored to a dock, Ivy adjusted her hat and tucked the errant hair underneath it, hoping she didn't look too disheveled. Merritt opened the basket door for her and held it open, waiting for her to step outside. It was a small gesture, but welcome.

When was the last time a man held open a door for her?

He even held out his arm for her. Despite her clothing announcing her status to the world, she couldn't keep herself from placing a gloved hand around him. No one who worked the docks would care. She was acutely aware of the feel of his arm through their layers of clothes. It was the closest she'd been to anyone since Edwin died, not that their marriage had been especially physically affectionate. Despite that fact, guilt threaded through her at the small pleasure she felt at the contact. She sneaked a glance at him.

He gave her a small smile, and her heart lifted a little at the sight.

It was a short walk to the Thaddeus bottling factory, the smallest of the warehouses that populated the Albert Dock area. Like the other buildings, its exterior was grimy with the soot and dirt endemic to this part of the city. It was a sharp contrast to its clean and tidy shop floor. Merritt's brows raised when they walked into the factory and he saw the great steam-powered bottling apparatuses, proprietary technology that Edwin commissioned when he turned his focus patent medicine. The crisp smell of herbs hung in the air, the scent amplified by the humidity issued by the bottling machines and assembly line. A few workers waited at intervals on the line, checking bottles.

Ivy released a breath she hadn't realized she was holding when she sensed that her magic still clung to the place. Her spells over the shop floor were still intact, imbuing the elixir with its pain-relief properties. Judging by Merritt's wide-eyed reaction, he could pick up on it, too.

"You have three ghosts hanging about here," he whispered in her ear.

Perhaps it wasn't the magic, after all. "Is Edwin among them?"

"I doubt it. They're all women, wearing fashions from the last century. I think they're friends or sisters." He paused, his head tilting to the side for a few seconds as if listening to someone. "Dearest friends, one has just informed me." His lips thinned. "I'm not here to exorcise you," he muttered. "Carry on as you were before."

"I didn't know the factory was haunted."

"They mean the living no harm." The irritated look on his face didn't leave. "Is there somewhere we could talk in private?"

Ivy inclined her head to an alcove. "Edwin's office is upstairs. It's been untouched since he died." She led him along the room to it, where staircases branched off in either direction. One led to the offices on the second floor. The other to supply rooms, full of herbs and empty bottles. She had been back at the factory a handful of times in the last year and a half, arriving at night to cast her spells. It felt odd to be here in the light of day, and even odder to know after all these years that the factory was haunted. As she closed Edwin's office door behind them, she couldn't help but ask, "Did they follow us?"

Merritt shook his head. "They just want to be left alone."

"Why are they here?"

"They didn't say, only that this space was their home and they mean no harm."

"It's incredible that spirits can see what you are so quickly."

He shrugged. "I've been told that necromancers and fae alike stand out to them. Claudia once told me I look like I have a halo. Anyway, the ladies downstairs were quick to tell me that they're minding their own business."

Even though she was supposed to be concerned about her husband's death, Ivy's curiosity about Merritt's ability was still piqued. "How old are they?" She hoped they'd had a chance to grow up and live out a reasonable span of years.

Merritt looked amused at the question. "They didn't say, they just wanted to know if I was there to evict them. They were adults, though. Perhaps around their forties."

Older than Ivy, then, although she often didn't feel like an adult at thirty-eight. She was relieved to hear that the ghosts at least had a chance at adulthood. She longed to ask more questions about them, but stopped herself. "This was Edwin's office," she said, gesturing around the space. Like his study at their home, it was tidy and well-kept. The desk drawers were locked, but a quick spell cast under her breath unlocked them.

Relief suffused her. Now that she was away from the house, her magic had returned.

She caught Merritt's impressed expression, and she couldn't keep herself from smiling. She'd felt like the most useless witch in existence recently. "I wouldn't have been able to do that at my house. There's certainly something there keeping me from my magic." Ivy removed a leather-bound folder and set it on the desktop. "Here's a copy of Edwin's will. It's the exact same copy on file with his solicitor, naming me as his primary beneficiary." She pushed the papers across the desk to Merritt's side.

Merritt sat in the chair in front of the desk before picking up the will. He leaned back, reading it.

Not knowing what else to do, Ivy took a seat in Edwin's chair. She opened other drawers, the contents unchanged since his death. She spotted a silver pocket watch she knew contained a small daguerreotype of his first wife. It was tarnished, the Lang Timepieces logo nearly blackened. She removed it and slipped it into her skirt pocket, intending to give it to Ezra the next time he showed up at her house uninvited.

She didn't speak until Merritt set aside the will. "What do you think?"

He shrugged. "Your husband isn't here."

Even though Ivy already knew that Edwin's spirit was blocked somehow, she still hated to hear that Merritt couldn't sense him in the place he'd spent the most time at. "Does the will explain any motives?"

"Yes. Every person named in the will, including you, had motive to kill him based on how the bequests were allocated. You're the most obvious one."

She knew that, but it still stung. "It's usually the spouse."

"Sometimes it isn't. Ezra was left a sizeable trust fund and properties in very desirable neighborhoods, and his business partner was left fifty percent of the business's profits." His eyes met hers. "All of you had something to gain from Edwin's passing."

"Ezra didn't do it," Ivy protested.

"I considered that he could have been deflecting blame from himself, but murderers generally don't go about hiring private detectives for ungodly amounts for months after a death to point the finger elsewhere."

"Is he paying you an ungodly amount?"

"Five hundred pounds," Merritt replied. "Although this case hardly has me doing five hundred pounds' worth of work, thanks to whoever banished your husband's spirit to wherever he is."

"You have to free him," Ivy urged.

"That's just as important as finding out how and why

he really died." Merritt picked up a page of the will again and skimmed it. "Does Roger McCann know about your abilities?"

"No. That was strictly between me and Edwin."

"Why doesn't McCann own a share of the business itself? It seems odd that a partner wouldn't."

"Edwin hired him to take care of the accounts years ago and he ended up a manager of sorts. He offered to buy the business or at least a part of it about three years ago, but Edwin refused because of the magic involved."

"There are clauses in this will that require the recipe for the elixir to be followed to the letter in the event of Edwin's death."

"Of course. I've been back here a few times to cast spells over the ingredients, although it's been a few months since my last visit."

"How long does the magic last?"

Ivy shrugged. "I have talismans in the walls to hold the magic longer and the spells I use are very powerful. I've spelled the bottling machines, too. I could leave this place alone for perhaps five months before the spells' efficacy wore off."

"Edwin wasn't familiar with any other magic practitioners?"

"No."

"Does Roger McCann believe in magic?"

"I know he attended séances with the rest of the fashionable set for a time. I don't know if he actually believes in spiritualism, though. He and Edwin were partners years before Edwin showed up in my shop." Ivy racked her brain, trying to think about what she knew about Roger McCann. The man was around Edwin's age and very private. In her few interactions with him, he'd always been polite but aloof. "Do you think he could have killed Edwin?"

"I can't tell yet." Merritt set the will down on the desktop. "A lot of this would be easier if I could just speak to your husband and find out what happened."

"Is that how you usually deal with murders?"

"When I still consulted with the police, yes."

"Why aren't you a constable?"

A wry smile crossed his face. "My methods aren't exactly sanctioned by humans. I could hardly tell anyone that I was asking murder victims directly how they came to die and who killed them. I prefer working for myself, including investigating cases where supernaturals are involved."

That bit of information took Ivy by surprise. "How frequently do witches and necromancers commit crimes?"

"Very rarely. I usually follow the trail of destruction caused by vampires before the human police forces can investigate. They're the most dangerous, by far."

Ivy was shocked. It took a moment for her to find her voice. "Vampires?"

He looked puzzled at her reaction. "You didn't know of them?"

"I didn't think they were real or if they were, common enough for a private detective to hunt them down!"

"I only hunt the ones who bother humans. I'm well-acquainted with a vampire who just wants to live out his unlife in peace with his human wife."

That answer only meant Ivy had more questions. "How does a vampire take a human wife?"

Merritt's expression shifted to one of... was it embarrassment? Color touched his cheeks. "It's a ritual that vampires and their familiars follow. I've never felt the need to ask for the specifics. He keeps his fangs to himself and his wife. That's all I'm concerned about."

Merritt spoke of the existence of vampires so casually that Ivy couldn't believe it. She had dozens more questions to ask him, not the least of which was a request to meet his vampire friend. Did they have tells that identified them as such? How many vampires had she passed in the street, oblivious to what they were?

He stood up and changed the subject. "Does McCann spend his days at the factory?"

Ivy nodded. Disappointment twanged through her at the shift in their conversation, but he was here to do a job unrelated to vampires. "His office is at the opposite end of the corridor. He doesn't have to account for his time to me, but he's likely to be here." She tilted her head to the side, curious. "What are you going to tell him? I can hardly act as if I brought you here for fun."

"A modified version of the truth. I've been hired to investigate your husband's death by your stepson and I suspect he may have actually been murdered. We'll gauge his reaction then."

"I see." She reminded herself that Merritt knew what he was doing, that there had to be good reasons for him speaking to her husband's business partner in such a manner.

Merritt straightened his hat brim. "It's time to pay a visit to McCann."

# CHAPTER 6

THE TRIO of friends who haunted Thaddeus Bottling Works left Merritt alone, for which he was grateful. His heart sank when he first saw them chatting together on the opposite end of the factory floor, and one of them sailed to him faster than he'd ever seen a ghost move to tell him to leave their home. She'd put on a false sense of bravado, her tall white wig's curls bobbing as she shook with nerves, that only evaporated when Merritt told her he wasn't there to exorcise them.

As he followed Ivy down the corridor to Roger McCann's office, he wondered why the three of them clung to this part of the mortal plane. At least they weren't lonely.

The door to McCann's office was open, revealing a man Merritt guessed to be in his late sixties sitting behind a desk. At Ivy and Merritt's appearance in his doorway, his dour expression brightened. "Mrs. Thaddeus! What a pleasant surprise, seeing you about."

"Hello," Ivy replied. "May we come in?"

"Of course." McCann gave a quick, inscrutable look in

Merritt's direction. "I don't think we've met before," he said. "Roger McCann."

"Merritt Sloan." He closed the short distance between them to shake McCann's proffered hand. The man's grip was cool and firm, belying his age. "I'm a private investigator. Ezra Thaddeus has hired me to investigate the late Dr. Thaddeus's death."

McCann sighed. "Is he still on about his father being murdered? Ezra doesn't have the sense God gave a fly."

Merritt gave him a thin smile. "Senseless or not, I've been hired to do a job and I've found some inconsistencies, for lack of a better word, with the late doctor's passing."

McCann's eyes widened in surprise. His shocked expression quickly gave way to an appalled one. "What the devil do you mean? His heart failed when he was taking a turn about his gardens. It isn't unheard of for someone his age to pass in such a manner."

"Other evidence has recently appeared," Merritt replied.

"Of what nature?"

"I cannot say yet." Merritt kept his tone cool and impassive. It was exactly the kind he used when he told his incredulous superior officers who had killed someone and where to find the evidence. Sometimes they listened to him and arrested the murderer. Other times, they didn't.

McCann shook his head. "That isn't possible. Edwin's been dead for nearly two years! How could you possibly believe he was murdered after all this time?"

"As I've told you, I cannot say. I do have some questions to ask you."

"Should I have my solicitor present?"

Merritt stole a glance at Ivy.

One dark eyebrow rose for half a second. "Why would you need your solicitor present?"

"Isn't that protocol when being questioned as a murder suspect?"

"You're not a suspect." Lies. Merritt's senses were on full alert. "I want to ask you some questions about your relationship with Dr. Thaddeus. How long did you work together? Where did you meet?"

McCann's expression relaxed a little. He returned to his chair and gestured to Ivy to sit in the one opposite him. There wasn't another seat, so Merritt stood, his notebook at the ready as McCann described meeting Dr. Thaddeus some twenty years earlier. Dr. Thaddeus founded the company and developed the original formulas for the elixirs. McCann had prior experience in patent medicine and he marketed it.

"I did the best I could with what I had to work with," McCann explained. "The Miracle Elixir didn't perform especially well in the early years on account of Dr. Thaddeus wanting to keep laudanum out of the formula."

Merritt nodded. "I've been informed that the Miracle Elixir is renowned for its lack of laudanum."

"It would be even more effective if it could be added to the formula, as I told Edwin repeatedly." McCann gave a pointed look to Ivy. "I've tried to convince Mrs. Thaddeus to reformulate the Miracle Elixir, but she refuses."

"If nothing is broken, it doesn't need to be fixed. Edwin's will also had stipulations to that effect." Ivy's voice was cool and firm.

Merritt wondered how often the subject of reformulation arose.

"The Miracle Elixir is the fourth most popular patent medicine in England. With the addition of laudanum or something similar, it could be the most popular."

"And yet its competitors are reformulated, removed from the market altogether, or written about in the penny papers after someone dies from it. No, we're keeping the Miracle Elixir as it is. Our customers like its consistency."

A shadow crossed over McCann's face.

Merritt reminded himself of how little control he had over the company relative to Ivy. If Ivy was out of the picture, he could exert more control over Thaddeus Bottling Works and reformulate the Miracle Elixir as he saw fit, in addition to reaping all of its profits.

Ivy hadn't received any threats aside from her home being spelled or cursed. The only person who had been remotely threatening was her stepson, who appeared to have little interest or care for the company and was motivated by justice for his father's death. McCann's frustration with the patent medicine's formula only added to the mystery.

"Nevertheless, change is good," McCann said. "It's important to follow what the customers want, and what they want is an effective patent medicine that can relieve pain and induce sleep."

"It already does that."

"The valerian root concoction can be improved upon."

"It has been. I perfected the formula myself. It needed more valerian root." Ivy's voice rose a little and he wondered how often they had had this argument since Dr. Thaddeus died. "The formula will not be changed."

Valerian root and a touch of magic, Merritt supposed.

Movement caught his eye in the opposite corner of the room. A floating figure in century-old court dress and tall white wig balanced on her head materialized. It was the same ghost who had scolded him earlier. She unfurled a pink-painted fan and waved it under her chin. Was that a code? Was Merritt supposed to excuse himself and find a private spot to speak to a ghost? He met her gaze briefly, hoping she understood his reluctance to speak to her. She remained in place, patiently waiting. Hopefully, she would seek him out again before they left the factory, when he and Ivy could be alone again.

McCann's voice was tight when he spoke. "I'm a man of science and business. Dr. Thaddeus was a great innovator, but once he landed on an idea he was reluctant to alter it in any way. The public has changed over the years."

"The public is happy with my formula," Ivy said. Her shoulders slumped a little. "Could you please just speak to Mr. Sloan and answer his questions, instead of arguing with me again? The sooner this is resolved to Ezra's satisfaction, the sooner Mr. Sloan will leave us alone."

"Your stepson is a greedy, empty-headed fool."

"That may be, but he loved his father more than anything and I just want this to be over."

"Did Dr. Thaddeus have any enemies in business?" Merritt asked.

"Of course. You don't become successful without any."

"Do you have names?" Merritt's pencil hovered over a fresh page in his notebook.

McCann chuckled. "Every patent medicine manufacturer in England. Mrs. Thaddeus speaks the truth. While the Miracle Elixir is only the fourth most-popular medicine in England, its position as such is consistent. It's common for patent medicines to disappear after a few years, and the Miracle Elixir has been available for decades."

*Every fucking medicine maker in England*, Merritt scribbled. He fought the urge to snap the notebook shut and walk out in frustration. There had to be hundreds of makers, small and large scale.

The ghost waved her fan again and gave him a knowing look. Did she know something? Perhaps it was time to leave McCann's office. The man was as obstinate as a mule.

Merritt asked him a few more questions about the medicine's history before taking his leave. Without thinking, he offered his hand to Ivy to help her up. McCann blinked at the gesture but didn't comment on it, an unreadable expression in his eyes. Oh, hell. Merritt was fairly certain he'd just breached some kind of mourning etiquette.

Ivy looked surprised, too, but still accepted the help.

That provided a small measure of relief. Why it was so important he had Ivy's approval, he couldn't tell. He thanked McCann for his time and ushered Ivy out of the room, back to Dr. Thaddeus's office.

"What is the meaning of this?" Ivy whispered.

Her breath tickled the sensitive spot under his ear, sending a frisson of unexpected heat through him. He swallowed and hoped she didn't notice. "I'll tell you shortly," he replied when he found his voice. He closed the door behind them and waited, hoping the ghost would return and she wasn't just fucking with him.

A moment later, she appeared, her form opaque in places. She gave him a look that questioned his intelligence. "You didn't say you're here to look after Dr. Thaddeus," she said.

"You rushed away so quickly after telling me to get out that I didn't have the chance," Merritt replied.

Ivy looked at him blankly. "Who are you talking… oh, is it the ghost you said haunts the factory?"

"Could you tell her we don't haunt this place?" The ghost's voice was prim, the tone of a woman who was used to being obeyed. "Haunting implies fear and destruction. My friends and I go out of our way not to bother the living."

"They aren't haunting the factory," Merritt said to Ivy. "If they were haunting it, you would know." That answer seemed to mollify Ivy, who nodded. To the ghost, he said, "What shall I call you?"

"Minerva."

"Why are you helping me?"

"Because the sooner you have what you want from this factory, the sooner you'll leave and never return to exorcise us."

"Do you know anything about Dr. Thaddeus's death? I can't summon his spirit."

"Perhaps you're a poor necromancer." Minerva's full lips upturned in a smirk. Merritt had the distinct impression that she would have been the one in her circle to issue the cut direct and decide who to cast out of *le bon ton* when she was alive. Rude and ungracious under a veneer of civility afforded her by the status of which she was born.

"His spirit has been cast into some kind of purgatory," Merritt explained, voice even.

"Can't you fish him out?"

"No. I don't engage in the type of dark magic that can do such a thing. I suspect that Dr. Thaddeus's death wasn't a natural one and his spirit being locked away from the mortal and ghostly planes has confirmed that. Someone wants him out of the way."

"He and Mr. McCann fought quite a bit before he died, for at least six months. It was near daily."

Merritt turned to Ivy. "Did you know your husband and McCann argued constantly before he passed?"

Ivy's eyes widened. "No, Edwin never mentioned it. What are they saying?"

"It would have been easy to miss, when you're only here once every couple of months to chant over the lavender plants in the apothecary," Minerva said. "Those two were on their best behavior when Mrs. Thaddeus came calling."

"What is she talking about?" Ivy asked again.

"Mr. McCann employed the use of a medium shortly after Dr. Thaddeus died," Minerva said. She folded her fan with a snap and tucked it underneath her arm. Merritt thought she must've used it as a prop when alive, to emphasize her points. It was still effective in death.

"What?" Merritt said, louder than he intended. He immediately lowered his voice. "How could a medium do that?"

She shrugged. "Mediums, necromancers, all the same thing to us."

"What can I possibly offer you to keep you from being obtuse and difficult in answering my questions?"

Minerva narrowed her eyes at him and snapped open her fan. "I could just leave you alone and let you fumble your way through this investigation of yours."

Irritation flared in him at her obstinacy. "My apologies, my temper got the best of me. I differentiate between mediums and necromancers. Mediums are charlatans."

"This one wasn't. McCann escorted him into the factory and the medium chanted things to keep the ghost of the dead doctor away. I didn't hear the specifics. My friends and I hid as soon as we recognized him."

"You only told me to leave."

She gave a half-shrug, encumbered by the weight of her gown and its panniers and frills. "You don't have a bad essence to you."

"You may be interested to know that I'm part fae. Unseelie, as a matter of fact."

"You can scarcely tell. You don't have an aura of malevolence around you that McCann's medium did. We hid in the walls, so we didn't hear him too clearly. He recited a spell that he told McCann would keep Dr. Thaddeus's soul away from the factory. He also said he had other spells to cast at other places important to Dr. Thaddeus."

A glance at Ivy showed her expression to be a mask of confusion and frustration. "I think McCann is the reason you can't cast spells at your home," he said quietly. "According to Minerva, he hired a medium who practices dark magic."

Outrage suffused her features. "Why would he do that?" she asked, her voice a hoarse whisper.

"He wants full control of the factory," Minerva said, just as Merritt said, "The company."

"Why not do away with me? I'm standing in the way out his taking full control," Ivy pointed out.

"Perhaps he didn't wish to arouse suspicion. Healthy women your age seldom drop dead from heart failure like your husband did." To Minerva, Merritt asked, "Have you heard anything about Mrs. Thaddeus and McCann's plans with her?"

The ghost shook her head, then adjusted her wig. "Only that he cast spells around her house."

"Do you know if McCann knows she's a witch?"

"No. Shall I skulk about his office and find out?"

"You're offering to help us?" Merritt asked in surprise.

"*I'm* offering to help. I don't speak for my companions."

"But you would do that?"

"I can keep my ears out for you." Minerva waved her fan under her chin. "My companions are enamored of each other, and I often find myself bored. This will keep me occupied. If you return in a few days or weeks, I may have some new information for you."

"You wouldn't happen to have the medium's name, would you?"

"Of course not. I would've started off by telling it to

you. All I can say is he's about your height, perhaps ten years older than you, silver-haired, and he wore a dreadful purple overcoat with a muskrat fur hood." Disdain dripped from her voice like icicles. "He was very loud when he chanted, too."

"Do you remember the language he used to cast his spells?"

"Latin. I'm hardly fluent in it, but I recognize it when I hear it."

Merritt's heart sank. They weren't dealing with a medium, but a necromancer with dark magic spellcasting abilities. He glanced at Ivy, her face still a picture of confusion. "We have our work cut out for us," he said wearily, and scrubbed a hand over his face. "This is going to be difficult."

Twilight had fallen when Ivy returned to her house, the covered gardens enveloped in purple and gray shadows. Now that she'd had a chance to spend time at the factory, she could feel how much her magic was depleted at her own home.

When the ornithopter was landed, Merritt asked her, "Are you certain it will be safe to stay here tonight?"

It was as if he'd read her mind but Ivy wasn't about to be cowed out of her own home. "As safe as it could be, considering the circumstances." She reached for the passenger basket's door. Merritt put a proprietary hand over hers before she could let herself out.

"If what Minerva told me is true, and I have reason to believe it is, then someone has trapped your husband's soul. He may have murdered him, too. In fact, I'm certain he did and that McCann arranged it. Now that he knows you're suspicious of him, he may come after you."

It made sense, yet… "Wouldn't it look just as suspicious for something to happen to me so soon after I spoke to Mr. McCann?"

"He was surprised and dismayed at my investigation, and Minerva confirmed that he'd spoken to a necromancer. You've told me that McCann attended séances."

Minerva. The ghost who haunted the factory yet claimed she didn't. Ivy felt like an idiot. "Of course. I still don't think Mr. McCann would try to do something to me so soon, though."

"Desperate people take desperate measures. He wants full control of the company. Perhaps he was biding his time before making your death appear as an accident or natural causes."

"There would still be Ezra to consider. He would be entitled to my share of the company if I died."

"Ezra has no interest in it, you've also said that. He has nothing to hold him back from selling his part of it to McCann."

A chill slithered down Ivy's spine. "Ezra hates me, but I doubt he would do anything to harm me." The words felt hollow as she said them. Ezra had never cared for her, and that indifference had transformed into outright loathing since Edwin died. Did he hate her enough to kill her?

"I'm not sure he would, either. He loved and respected his father and believes he was murdered. He's the whole reason I'm here."

Ivy nodded and looked away, focusing on the house for a moment as she collected herself. A part of her was glad that Merritt was in her life now despite the circumstances. She had never had the chance to interact with other people with supernatural talents, other than the witches in her late mother's coven. It was nice to know someone else with magic. The feeling warred with guilt. She was still a widow in half-mourning. "When shall I see you again?" she asked. She was already looking forward to it. She tamped it down and hoped the anticipation didn't show on her face. *Professional*, she reminded herself. Merritt was a professional.

"I'm going to discreetly ask about mediums in the city," Merritt replied. "I'll have reports for you and Ezra within the next couple of days."

"Should I be paying you, too? I've been monopolizing your time since Ezra hired you."

Merritt paused.

"Is that a yes?"

"No," he said slowly, as if mulling over his words. "I was thinking that this might be a conflict of interest." He corrected himself. "It *is* a conflict of interest."

"I'm not the killer. Or soul stealer, whatever you call someone who boxes up spirits." The thought of Edwin trapped in purgatory made her heart ache.

Merritt's voice was soft. "I know, but your stepson hired me to prove that you are."

"He hired you to prove that my husband was murdered. He just happens to think that I did it."

He gave her a rueful smile that made her heart skip a beat.

Once upon a time, she would have thought he might have been trying to flirt with her. She told herself to get over that notion. Merritt was investigating her husband's murder. Besides that, she was older than him. Younger men didn't flirt with older women, especially ones still in widow's weeds. She unlatched the passenger basket's door and let herself out.

Merritt followed, offering his arm again. "Let me walk you to your home, at least. It's dark out."

"I've lived here for over a decade. I'm familiar with the grounds." Despite her protest, she accepted it. She had the feeling she would always take any opportunity he offered to touch him.

He slowed as they started up the hill's path to the house in a way that had nothing to do with its incline. "Something doesn't feel right about this," he murmured.

"Of course, it doesn't. Someone has muted spellcasting and magical abilities on site."

"That makes me nervous. It should make *you* nervous. How else would you defend yourself?"

"No one has come after me before," she said. Her voice was more curt than she intended. "I don't need magic to defend myself. I've always loved my life as a normal human woman first, who happens to have some magical abilities bestowed on me by nature and the goddess herself. You have to understand that the women who came before me *had* to live like that. I continue to, aside from my spells on the Miracle Elixir. Moreover, this is my home. I'm not leaving it." Indignation and frustration colored her words as her ire rose. "Both of us agreed that it would be foolish for Mr. McCann or the medium he hired to come after me in some way. I will be fine for now."

He didn't reply, but the muscles in his arm tensed under her.

She knew it was from irritation, maybe even anger at her stubbornness, but it had an effect on her all the same. She felt herself flush and she was very glad for the darkness around them.

The only sound was that of their boots against the path's cobblestones, until Merritt uttered, "Fuck, no." He halted so suddenly Ivy nearly stumbled.

"What is it?" Already on edge, her heart thundered against her ribs.

"It's your housekeeper. Martha." Rage cut through his voice.

She was about to say that Martha was in the house, but stopped herself. She went numb. Had she not been holding on to his arm, Ivy might have fallen over. Her stomach lurched and she thought she might be sick on the cobbles. Tears sprang to her eyes. She already knew the answer, yet she still had to ask. "What are you saying?"

His next words were clipped in anger. "Her spirit's right in front of us. She's dead."

# CHAPTER 7

MERRITT DESPERATELY WISHED he could take his leave Ivy's house and take her with him, but he couldn't. Nor would he leave her alone. He couldn't leave her to the vultures currently investigating Martha's murder, as half-arsed as their investigation was. Nor could he leave Martha, who stayed near him and turned her nose up at every word the investigating officer from the Liverpool force uttered.

Merritt had briefly spoken with Sergeant Thompson before he stopped his consultations with the police. After ten minutes of poking about the house and her body, Thompson declared that Martha had taken a fall down the stairs, breaking her neck in the process, and that her death was simply a tragic accident.

"Bollocks," Martha muttered next to Merritt.

It was after midnight when the local undertaker collected Martha's body and the police left the house. Ivy sat on an overstuffed chair in the sitting room off the foyer, hands clenched together in her lap so tightly her knuckles were white. Her gaze was trained on the floor as her shoulders shook with silent sobs. The urge to take her into his arms and try to comfort her was overwhelming, but Merritt didn't move.

"He mistook me for Mrs. Thaddeus. I'm sure of it," Martha said.

Merritt had hardly had a chance to speak with Martha directly since her ghost appeared to them on the cobblestone path. Between summoning the police, a task undertaken by the groundskeeper who lived in a cottage on the opposite side of the property, and the need to preserve the crime scene exactly, Merritt hadn't been able to sit down and speak to Martha. The dead housekeeper had yelled at Thompson to no avail as the sergeant declared her death an obvious accident. Now, they had time. The groundskeeper had offered up the use of his cottage to Ivy, who refused, before he left for the night.

Martha glanced at Ivy, then Merritt. "Should we leave her be before we talk?"

"Ivy," said Merritt gently. She looked up, eyes red and tear tracks running down her cheeks. "Martha wants to know if you're comfortable with me speaking to her here."

Ivy looked insulted at the notion. "Of course I am!" She sniffled and dabbed at her eyes with a sodden handkerchief. "Don't mind me. She's a lovely woman. I'm sorry this happened to her."

Now it was Martha's turn to wipe away tears. "Can you tell her I appreciated our years of companionship and I'll miss her dearly?"

Merritt nodded, his own throat closing a little at the desolation in her voice. "Martha asked me to tell you that your years together were valued and she'll miss you."

"She won't haunt the house? I wouldn't mind if she did," Ivy quickly added. "I want her to be happy wherever she goes."

"I'll be moving on shortly," Martha replied as if Ivy

could hear her. Her voice broke. "I can feel the pull of the afterlife from here, and it's like a sunny day at the beach. I'll see my parents and grandparents again. My Charlie's there, too. He's been waiting for me for years." To Merritt, she said, "Tell her I'm sorry I won't be here anymore. I can't stay. I don't want to hang about while no one is punished for killing me."

The fury that rose in him shoved aside his grief. "I'll be investigating this myself. I promise, I'll find out who did this to you and see that he pays for it."

"They're calling me," Martha said. Her voice was distant and distracted. "I'll have to make this quick. There isn't much to tell."

Merritt slipped his notebook from his pocket and opened it to a fresh page. "Tell me."

"I was at the top of the stairs, my hand on the banister, when I heard the front door open," Martha began. "I thought it might have been Mrs. Thaddeus, but she always announces herself when she opens the door and it always bangs against the jamb. She likes to make an entrance." Martha gave a sad smile to Ivy, who stared in Martha's direction without actually looking at her. "It was opened quietly and I didn't hear Mrs. Thaddeus. I thought it might have been Mr. Thaddeus and called out to him, but I didn't hear an answer. You can see the foyer from the third stair, but only the floor. I could only see an unfamiliar pair of dark trousers and boots, not in Mr. Thaddeus's style at all." She took a watery breath and looked at Ivy's skirt before continuing. "I went down a couple more stairs before it felt like the air changed. I don't know how to describe it. Something pushed and pulled me at the same time. I felt invisible hands wrap around my neck and choke me. I remember falling down the stairs and hearing a... a crunch in my neck." Her voice broke.

Merritt closed his eyes and breathed deeply, trying to keep his heartbeat under control. Hearing about murders from the victims themselves would never not have an impact on him.

Martha continued after a moment. "The next thing I knew, I was standing over myself, looking at my own body with my neck bent at an angle."

"Did you get a good look at the man?" Merritt asked quietly.

"I'm not sure how tall he was. Shorter than Dr. Thaddeus's son. Built broader, too, but not by much. He had hair gone gray, but his face didn't match. Too young for it, but I wasn't thinking about his age when I realized I was dead. He cursed when he looked at me, then walked out of the house."

Minerva had mentioned a silver-haired man. It sounded like his most distinguishing feature. "Thank you," he said. "That's been very helpful."

"Do you know him?" Martha asked sharply.

"No, we've only been made aware of his existence today." Considering the late hour, technically it was yesterday. "Martha, I'm so sorry this happened to you."

She wiped her eyes and sniffled. "Not your fault. I'd like to leave now. Charlie's calling me."

"May I call on you at a later time, if I have anything to ask?"

"As long as I don't get stuck here, I don't see why not." She took a deep breath and steeled herself. She placed a hand on Ivy's shoulder, causing her to jump.

"Martha?" Ivy breathed, looking around.

Martha's voice was soft. "I'm not happy about our parting being this way, either." She tilted her head to the side, as if listening to someone. She likely was. "I'm sure we'll cross paths again someday. Goodbye, Mrs. Thaddeus." She stepped away from Ivy and nodded at Merritt before her form vanished.

Ivy turned her tear-streaked face to Merritt. "What did she say?"

He looked at the spot where Martha's ghost was only a moment before. Sadness enveloped the room like a wool blanket on a hot night. "She crossed over. Before she left, she said that she wished your parting could have been under better circumstances and she'll see you again in the afterlife. She has people waiting for her there." Curiosity pulled at him. "Did she ever tell you about a fellow named Charlie?"

"He was her beau when they were younger. He died when he was around twenty."

"She said he was calling her."

Ivy let out a sob and pressed her handkerchief to her eyes. "She rarely spoke of him, but when she did it was plain that she adored him. I hope they can finally be together." She looked at the doorway that led to the foyer. The place where Martha's body was found couldn't be seen from her spot on the chair, but Merritt knew what she was thinking about. "I wish it could have been under better circumstances, too. My God, she was killed because of me!"

"This wasn't your fault," Merritt said, but she interrupted him.

She shook her head. "Yes, it was. Whether it was a case of mistaken identity or she was killed as a warning, Martha would still be alive if it wasn't for me. If I'd done something to reinforce my protection spells around the house, she might still be alive."

"Do you know other witches who could help you with those spells?" Merritt asked gently.

"No. We don't have covens in England the way we did

hundreds of years ago. The only person I could ask about spells are my sister." She leaned back in her chair, her shoulders slumping. "She replied to my cable. I forgot to tell you, not that it would have helped anyway, because she isn't familiar with dark magic. You wouldn't happen to know anyone who could cast spells, would you?"

"No, but my parents know a thing about dark magic."

"Ah, yes. Your half-fae mother and father."

Merritt had never asked for help from his parents with a case, and he felt his heart sink when he realized he might have to do that, if he couldn't locate McCann's medium. "If it comes to that, we'll pay them a visit. They know more about dark magic than I do."

"Why didn't you raise her from the dead?"

The question came out of nowhere, taking Merritt by surprise. "I'm sorry?" He'd already told her he wouldn't do that. He hadn't done that since he was a boy, before he could control his powers.

"You're a necromancer. Why didn't you bring Martha back to life? She had just died. Perhaps she would have had a chance."

He sat down in the chair opposite hers. He moved it closer to Ivy's, then reached for her hands. He was relieved when she twined her fingers around his, accepting his touch. He chose his words carefully. "She wouldn't have been the same."

"You mean her neck would still have been broken."

He nodded. "She wouldn't have been able to resume her life as it was. A necromancer can only keep a dead person alive for a short time. It requires a tremendous amount of power and energy to do that. I could never do that to Martha or anyone. No one wants to return to a dead body."

Somewhere in the house, a clock struck one o'clock.

"Get some sleep," Merritt suggested. "In the morning, you'll pack a bag and we'll leave the house. It's for your own safety. I have no doubt that whoever killed Martha will return."

"What about you?"

Warmth spread through him at her concern. "I'll stay here."

"Let me fix up a bedroom for you."

"No, I'll stay here, in view of the front door. I won't be sleeping."

"Do necromancers need less sleep?"

"No, but I can stay awake to make sure no one tries to enter the house again."

She stood up, breaking their contact. He immediately missed it, and then dismissed that notion. It was inappropriate. "I'll take the servants' stairs," she said. She looked at the foyer and shuddered.

Merritt understood. "I'll be here."

Ivy TOSSED and turned in between snatches of light sleep, unable to get the image of Martha's body out of her mind. Tears wet her pillow as guilt crashed through her. Martha had been Edwin's housekeeper before he married Ivy. In recent months the two had grown closer than employer and employee. Martha knew what it was to lose someone tragically, even though she'd only spoken of her late Charlie a handful of times. The knowledge that the two of them were now together wasn't as much of a comfort to Ivy as it probably should have been.

It was still dark out when six o'clock rolled around, and she gave up trying to sleep. She crawled out of bed and set about packing in preparation for her flight from her home.

Would she even be safe away from here? The medium who killed Martha and presumably blocked her spellcasting abilities clearly had some powerful dark magic at his disposal. Not for the first time, Ivy wished her mother was still around to help her out with this.

She packed a bag and left it in the middle of the floor. Surveying her appearance in the room's full-length looking glass, she sighed. She looked and felt like she hadn't slept in days. Her unbound hair had frizzed and tangled from tossing side to side all night, her old dressing gown over-sized. Even in the dim light offered by the room's flameless candles, she could see the dark half-moons under her swollen eyes. She looked a mess. She supposed Merritt would have seen worse. She tightened the silk belt on the dressing gown and left the bedroom.

The private detective was sprawled on the velvet sofa in her sitting room, jacket off and sleeves rolled up, a book in his hands. His hat rested on the chair she sat in the night before, and his shoes were on the floor. She'd never seen him look so… normal. Relaxed. Including the time she knocked on his flat door when he was half-drunk and babbling to his resident ghost. For some stupid reason, the memory of that incident made her smile a little.

He was awake, though, and started when she appeared in the doorway. "Did you get any sleep?" he asked by way of greeting.

"Perhaps an hour's worth." She hovered in the door-way. "Shall I fix us some breakfast?"

"Allow me to help." He rose and set aside the book. "I hope you don't mind that I raided your late husband's bookshelves. It appears he was very fond of gardening."

He'd died in his gardens, collapsing on the burlap that protected his beloved rosebushes. "All the better for formulating medicine."

"A book about the cultivation of lavender was infinitely more interesting than anatomy, I must admit."

He followed her to the kitchen, where Ivy set a pot of water to boil for tea. She found a few scones in the bread-box, the last of a batch Martha had baked. Ivy felt her grief well up again as she set them out on a plate. "Is Martha here?"

Merritt sat at the table, a sad look on his face. "No."

"Are there any other ghosts? I've never thought to ask."

"No, your home is completely ghost-free."

Ivy had guessed as much, but it was nice to have that confirmed. She set out cups and measured tea leaves as she waited for the water to boil. A hurried knock at the front door nearly had her dropping the tea tin. "What now?" she muttered.

Merritt was already on his feet, skulking along the floor to the front door like he wanted to sneak up on someone.

Ivy followed close behind. "It's probably Ezra," she said. She recognized his knock, just as she knew he would unlock the door and let himself in without bothering to wait for her or Martha to open the door.

True to form, the door slammed open. "Ivy!" Ezra bellowed.

Ivy pushed past Merritt to the foyer. Her gorge rose when she saw the spot where Martha fell and she peeled her eyes away to face her stepson. His expression was ashen.

He knew. He had to.

"What's this I've heard about Martha?" he demanded. Despite the boom in his voice, Ivy heard the crack in it. He had known Martha since he was a boy.

Ivy had hoped to be controlled, to deliver the news of Martha's death as matter-of-factly as possible. A lump formed in her throat and she had to fight to get the words out. "It's true. We found her last night."

"What the hell happened?" Before Ezra could answer, he noticed Merritt. "Sloan! What the hell are you doing here at this time?"

"I could hardly leave Mrs. Thaddeus alone in such a time as this."

Ezra looked like he wanted to argue with Merritt over his presence, but didn't. "What happened to Martha?"

"Who told you?" Ivy asked.

"I received a visit from a *Mercury* reporter at half-five this morning. I suppose he wanted to catch me unawares."

Ivy had nearly forgotten about what the press could be like. They had hounded her for days after Edwin's death. The passing of a well-known wealthy older man would always bring unwanted attention to their younger wives. "I'm sorry," she said.

"How did the newspaper know Martha was dead?" Ezra demanded.

"How the hell do you think?" Merritt snapped. "They keep policemen on their payroll. Unexpected deaths and gruesome crimes sell papers."

"Martha's death was the result of a gruesome crime?"

Ivy caught Merritt's eye, but his expression was unreadable. "The police and the undertaker said it was an accident," she said quietly. "She fell down the stairs."

"Yes, I gathered that from the reporter." Ezra's voice broke and he turned away for a moment. Ivy did so, too, to give him some privacy.

From the kitchen, Ivy heard the kettle whistling. "Excuse me."

She hurried away, not wanting to be in the foyer any longer, and poured water over tea leaves into her favorite pot. Merritt and Ezra's voices murmured in conversation, then rose a little before Ezra shouted at him to get out of his father's house. The door slammed shut.

Ivy's stomach turned over. What now?

A few minutes later, a sheepish Merritt returned to the kitchen.

"What is it?" Ivy asked.

"Oh, well." He picked up a scone and buttered it. "Your stepson has just sacked me."

# CHAPTER 8

WEAK SUNLIGHT BROKE through the early morning gray sky when Merritt and Ivy left the house. He secured her bags into his ornithopter's passenger basket, and over her protests accompanied her to the groundskeeper's cottage to urge him to leave. Her protests were halfhearted. She knew how dangerous it was for her right now. Her home was no longer safe. The groundskeeper promised to leave that day after he checked the shrubbery's canvas covers, telling them he would stay with his brother in Liverpool.

Ivy hadn't stopped apologizing to Merritt, either, for his losing the case. "It's quite all right," Merritt kept trying to reassure her. "He still paid me one hundred pounds and no one would have blamed him if he hadn't."

"Did he say why he sacked you? Exactly how quickly did he expect you to solve it?" She adjusted her hat over her hair before stepping into the ornithopter's passenger basket.

Merritt hesitated. "He dismissed me because I spent the night here."

She turned stricken eyes to him. "My housekeeper died last night! There must be more to it!"

She was right, of course. "He didn't care for my having spent so much time with you."

"You're investigating my husband's death."

"I'm investigating his father's death," he gently corrected her. "He didn't like how I approached this case. He suspects us of having been, well, improper." He felt like an idiot saying the word. They were both adults. What did proper behavior matter to a widow and a private detective? No one cared what people of their ages and statuses—or lack of one, in Merritt's case—got up to.

No one except Ezra, unfortunately.

"Well, I'll hire you for myself," Ivy said. "Consider yourself back on the case. You're to find out who killed Edwin and then free his soul."

Merritt had been thinking about how to best approach that. "I believe I'll have to pay a visit to my parents for that." He slipped his goggles over his eyes and handed a matching pair to Ivy, who did likewise. He wound a lever on the ornithopter's navigation to start its engine. The sound of steam faintly hissed through the still air and the basket jerked a little as it the conveyance as it rose in the air, fighting gravity.

"I'll pay you the rest of the five hundred pound fee, plus expenses, of course."

"My fee isn't actually five hundred pounds. I would be living in a nicer house and have hired a housekeeper if it was. Your stepson wanted me to prioritize this case over everything else and devote as many waking minutes to it as I could."

"Did he think offering more money would get it solved faster?"

"Possibly, and when clients offer such a large amount

it's also to ensure that I'm at their beck and call whenever they want." As the ornithopter took off, he changed the subject. "Where did you plan on staying for the time being?"

She adjusted her goggles before replying. "The Adelphi Hotel. I've stayed there before."

"You don't have any family or friends to stay with?"

"My parents are deceased and my sister is too far away. I don't have any friends I would want to put in danger on my behalf. I'll be fine at the hotel." She gave him a tight smile.

That was probably the best place for her to stay, and yet… something squeezed in Merritt's chest. A part of him had hoped she might want to stay with him, in his flat. She would be safe with him, and Claudia would alert him to any dangers as soon as they approached the front door. He reminded himself that she was so far beyond his station in life, out of his element, that wishing for such a thing was futile. She had five hundred pounds to throw about on a whim, more than he would earn in years. He shook his head, as if to clear away those foolish thoughts. Ivy Thaddeus was a client, and it was inappropriate for a client to stay with him. He was a necromancer and private detective, not a guard. He didn't even have his clockwork pistol on him.

However, Ivy once sought him out at his flat. Did that count for something?

The flight back to the city was quick, and they traveled in silence. The air was crisp, an autumn bite to it that reminded Merritt that he would soon have to haul out his heavier coat from storage. As it was, he noticed Ivy shivering a little at his side. She held her arms around herself in an attempt to ward off the chill. If Merritt had his own coat handy and it wouldn't be a completely improper gesture between a client and employer, he would have offered it to her like the gentleman he wasn't.

The Adelphi Hotel had a ground level dock for ornithopters, and Merritt guided it there. Over Ivy's protests, he helped her with her bags to the front desk and waited while she reserved a room. He let the hotel's bellhop handle her bags, and they walked behind him as he led them to her fourth-floor room. "Get some rest," Merritt said quietly.

She gave a soft snort at that suggestion. "I can't see myself having a good night's sleep any time soon." Something must have shown on his face, because she quickly added, "I shall try. You need some sleep, too. Why don't we meet this afternoon and we'll decide what to do next?"

Merritt wanted to go back to the bottling factory and speak to Minerva or her companions, but didn't want to agitate Roger McCann. "I would like to speak to my parents."

She nodded. "They would have more knowledge about dark magic than either of us?" She whispered the words into Merritt's ear, which shouldn't have had the effect on him that it did.

"Only of it. Their knowledge is entirely theoretical and a good jumping off point for us, I think."

The bellhop opened the door with a brass key and held it for them. He handed the key to Ivy before bowing his head and leaving them alone.

Ivy unpinned her hat and set it on the room's writing desk. She rubbed the spot where her neck met her shoulder, and for a few seconds Merritt wished he could be the one doing that for her. "My flat isn't far from here. If you need anything, stop by it or my office if I'm not there. It's in Nelson Street."

"I didn't know you had an office."

"I'm rarely there."

She pulled out a couple of the pins that held her hair in a knot at the base of her neck and rubbed the back of her head.

It shouldn't have been alluring as it was. Merritt looked away before he could stare and make an idiot out of himself. They were both sleep-deprived. Ivy had experienced a terrible loss and shock the night before.

What the hell was wrong with him? He prided himself on his professionalism, his detachment to such sights. "I'll return at half two," he said. He glanced at his pocket watch. "That gives us five and a half hours to get a nap. We'll visit my parents together and hear what they have to say about trapping souls."

"Oh, God, I've been thinking about poor Martha all night and forgot that my husband's trapped in purgatory." Ivy closed her eyes, as if she was willing away tears. She probably was.

"Ivy." Merritt moved a little closer to her, his gaze catching hers. Her eyes were bloodshot with exhaustion and unshed tears, the circles beneath them pronounced. She was still the most beautiful woman he'd ever seen. He tamped down that feeling. "We'll find out what happened to them and I promise that we'll free your husband's spirit." He hoped like hell he could pull that off.

"I know, but…" Ivy trailed off. "Don't make promises you can't keep."

"I'm not. If someone's spirit can be trapped, it can be freed. There isn't an action in magic that can't be undone."

"It can be held if a practitioner doesn't have the skills or knowledge to undo it. Look, I don't want to argue with you on this front." She pasted a smile to her face, but it didn't reach her eyes. "I will try to take a nap, and I'll meet you in the hotel lobby at half two."

~

IN THE CONFINES of her rented room, Ivy was finally able to get some sleep. She only managed to slumber away a couple of hours, but woke feeling as if she slept all night. She hoped to maintain that energy the rest of the day.

She washed and dressed in one of her two half-mourning ensembles, noting that she was only obligated to wear them for another couple of months. She missed wearing colors and fabrics other than black, lavender, and gray, bombazine and crepe. By the winter, her mourning period would be over and could return to wearing her wardrobe of velvets and silks, their jewel-toned colors bright.

Her hat pinned to her hair, she left the room. She hesitated in the corridor for a moment before casting a spell over the room to keep the door locked. It felt good to have full access to her magic again, and she cursed herself for not noticing its hindrances back at her home.

Merritt was already in the lobby, his back to her as he surveyed the afternoon crowd going in and out of the hotel.

She would have recognized that form anywhere: while his clothes were serviceable, there was an aura of quiet strength and authority around him, something about him that announced that he was dependable, a friend to all who needed one. Of course, the view of his backside wasn't one to dismiss, either. Ivy let herself indulge in the sight before he turned around. She quickly raised her glance to his face, feeling heat rise to her cheeks. At least he looked better rested than this morning. "Good afternoon," she said.

"Afternoon to you, too. We'll take a steam cab to my parents' home. They aren't too far from here." He smiled and offered her his arm, gestures she didn't think she could ever tire of.

Just as quickly, her feelings shifted as she remembered why they were visiting his parents. The thought of Martha and Edwin made something in her chest twist, as did the notion that she was increasingly attracted to Merritt. She was still in mourning, after all. Even if she wasn't, she had to be nearly a decade his senior.

He hailed a steam cab and helped her into the backseat, taking the spot next to her after he gave the driver directions.

She watched the city go by through the cab's grimy windows, noting how long it had been since she visited Liverpool proper. Little had changed in her absence, other than the increased amount of dirt that covered everything.

The cab brought them to a quiet side street in St. Helens, to a row of well-kept, narrow brick houses with tiny gardens in front. After helping her out of the vehicle and paying the driver, Merritt opened the wooden gate of one of the houses. Its postage stamp-sized garden was covered over with burlap, not unlike her own gardens at home, and she wondered what Merritt's parents grew when the weather was fine.

Merritt raised the brass knocker on the front door, but before he could let it drop, the bolt on the other side scraped against the wood. The door opened to reveal a plump woman with blond hair streaked with silver, pinned in a knot on the back of her head. Her house dress was faded blue cotton, with an apron over it. "I thought you'd be visiting today," she said by way of greeting, beaming at Merritt.

"It's nice to see you, Mother. This is my friend, Mrs. Ivy Thaddeus."

Ivy nodded and held out her hand. Mrs. Sloan didn't

accept it, her gray eyes instead searching Ivy's face. She felt herself flush and dropped her hand back to her side. She glanced at Merritt, who looked as flummoxed as she felt.

Ivy was fairly certain why his mother was acting the way she was. "I'm a witch," she explained.

Understanding dawned on the older woman's face. "I see. I haven't met many in my time." She stepped aside. "Come on in. I was just about to put some tea on."

A knot of anxiety that Ivy hadn't realized she was holding between her shoulders unfurled itself, and she followed Merritt into the house. "Your sister's expecting again," Mrs. Sloan called over her shoulder. "Sometime in early spring, she thinks."

"You have a sister?" Ivy asked.

Merritt doffed his hat and tucked it under his arm. "Julia lives in Manchester with her family."

"Five children," Mrs. Sloan said in wonder. "Well, almost six. I don't know how she does it. Merritt's father and I could hardly get by with two."

The house's corridors were narrow, the rooms small and cheerfully decorated. The foyer led to a sitting room, where a staircase to the second floor was visible next to a doorway that revealed a kitchen. The sitting room's walls were draped with ancient-looking hand-stitched tapestries depicting winged fairies in different scenes, many of them violent. A few oil paintings of field scenes were displayed, all signed with the same looping script that read *Angus Sloan.*

"Your father's visiting with his friends for a chess match or some such thing. He'll be sorry he missed you." Mrs. Sloan said from the kitchen. She returned to the sitting room bearing a scarred wooden tray, a dented tin teapot and mismatched cups balanced on it. She set it on the table in the middle of the room, then gestured to the settee in front of it. "Sit."

It sounded like an order. Ivy and Merritt obeyed.

"Is Father's chess improving?" Merritt asked.

"He's still enjoying it, so I suppose so. He doesn't lose quite so often." She poured cups for all three of them. To Ivy, she said, "My husband has taken up a few hobbies in his retirement." She looked pointedly at the wall of oil paintings. She leaned back in her chair and took a long pull from her cup. "What brings you two here?"

"Mrs. Thaddeus's home has been cursed and her late husband's spirit is trapped," Merritt replied bluntly.

The news didn't seem to faze Mrs. Sloan. "That's a hell of a pickle to be in."

"I think this has been caused by a necromancer using dark magic."

"Of course it would be. The question is whether the necromancer is using fae or witch magic." Mrs. Sloan's gaze turned back to Ivy. "What kind of witch are you?"

"I don't practice dark magic at all. I'm more interested in apothecary sciences."

"Mrs. Thaddeus's late husband was the founder of Dr. Thaddeus's Miracle Elixir," Merritt explained. "He passed on nearly two years ago from what was originally ruled to be natural causes, but we have reason to believe he was murdered. His soul is trapped and I've been unable to free him." His last words were tinged with embarrassment.

"You've never had that problem before."

"I know, which is why I'm here today."

Mrs. Sloan finished off the rest of her tea in a few gulps, then poured another cup. "There are spells that can be cast to free a soul trapped by someone else, but they're risky and you need strong spellcasting abilities in the first place."

"I can do that," Ivy volunteered. "I *want* to. Edwin doesn't deserve to be trapped in purgatory."

Mrs. Sloan regarded her thoughtfully for a moment. "I've never cast spells myself, and the ones I have are old and very dark magic. They're dangerous."

"So is whoever trapped the late Dr. Thaddeus. Ivy's housekeeper was murdered last night while she was away," Merritt said.

Mrs. Sloan lifted an eyebrow in response to his using Ivy's given name, her only reaction to it. "Did you speak to this housekeeper?"

"Yes, before she left this plane. She described her killer, which matches the description of a man seen in the company of the late Dr. Thaddeus's business partner. We don't have his name and I was hoping you may have heard of a medium who looks like him."

"I refuse to associate with mediums and their nonsense."

"So do I, but this man isn't another charlatan pretending to speak to the dead. He's a true necromancer and very dangerous," Merritt pressed. "We know he's about my height, silver-haired, and slender."

"That's half the men in Liverpool. That's your *father*. In another ten years it'll be you."

"Have you heard of any mediums of extraordinary talents, Mother?"

"No, as I said. I would take a look around the city center and see who's advertising the séance shows, find out if there are any mediums of that description." Mrs. Sloan shrugged. "I'm sorry I can't be of more help."

Ivy couldn't help but ask, "What about the spells?"

"I have copies of those around here." She gulped another mouthful of tea before speaking again. Merritt and Ivy had barely touched theirs. "I mean no disrespect to you, but I'd rather not pass those on to someone of your abilities. I'm part fae with some witch blood in me from few generations back and I'm too frightened to use them, myself."

"Ivy is a capable witch," Merritt said.

"I'm sure she is, with plants and cooking spells."

The remark stung, but Ivy knew Mrs. Sloan was correct. Ivy had never used her magic for anything more nefarious than improving the taste of an over-salted roast. "Do you know anyone familiar with dark magic?" she asked.

Mrs. Sloan looked at her like she had two heads before she replied. "No. If I'd wanted to mess about with those who can kill others with just a few words and a wiggle of their fingers, I would start associating with the unseelier side of the family."

"'Unseelier' isn't a word, Mother. Uncle John is more seedy than unseelie."

"The seelie fae had the sense not to breed themselves out of existence."

Merritt pinched the bridge of his nose between his fingers. "I said 'seedy,' which is an apt word for your book-maker of a brother, who I doubt would be much help in this case. We won't use the spells for evil purposes. There may be alternatives to them, if we can see the original incantations."

Mrs. Sloan looked at one of her husband's paintings as if it was the most interesting thing in the world. "I don't even know if they work."

Ivy thought she might be stalling. It took a few seconds for her to realize Merritt's mother was afraid: of the dark magic the spells contained, of Merritt's role in this investigation. She loved her son.

"Mother, please." Merritt's voice was gentle but firm.

"It's very important to Mrs. Thaddeus that her husband's spirit be freed and allowed to move on to the afterlife."

"Of course it would be." A noisy sigh escaped Mrs. Sloan. She set down her cup with a clatter. "It might just be easier to find out who this necromancer is and kill him to break the spell, all told."

The ease with which she said that startled Ivy. She exchanged a glance with Merritt, whose expression was one of frustration. "Do you make it a habit to kill people?" she couldn't help but ask.

"No. I'm just pointing out that it would be easier to do it that way. Merritt could make it look like an accident."

Ivy couldn't help but sneak another look at Merritt, whose lips had thinned. She couldn't read his expression otherwise.

"I'm not killing anyone," he said evenly. "If you can pass on those spells, we would appreciate that. If not, that's fine, as well."

"I'll get you the spells. I'm just telling you that it's dangerous magic." Mrs. Sloan got to her feet and shuffled to the stairs.

As if sensing an opportunity that could get away too quickly, Merritt quickly shifted to better face Ivy. "I'd like to swear that she isn't like this, but she is," he said, voice a whisper. "I was hoping she would be, well, normal while you're here, but it seems I was mistaken. She doesn't expect either of us to kill anyone, she's just very blunt."

Relief poured through her at that bit of news. "I see."

"We'll do as she suggests after we leave with the spells and look for mediums in Liverpool. There are any number of séances being held around the country at any given time. Damn it, I wish Minerva had more information about the one McCann hired."

"Perhaps he's returned to the bottling factory since," Ivy suggested.

"Perhaps there are notes in his office about the medium." Merritt's expression turned thoughtful. "Would you feel comfortable paying another visit to the factory after hours?"

"As long as I don't go alone."

"Of course, I would be with you." As if to drive his point home, he gave her a look that clearly questioned her about his intentions.

Something in her turned over, quivered, even though what sprang to her mind couldn't be his intention. Perhaps she felt like that because it had been so long since anyone cared about her.

The stairs creaked as Mrs. Sloan descended them. She returned to the sitting room with a small ancient-looking leather folder, which she handed to Merritt.

He gingerly opened it. "What is this?" he asked.

"Some kind of tanned skin. Perhaps a demon or an unseelie fae's? It was in your grandmother's family for years."

Merritt dropped it on the table as if it was a hot coal. A wave of disgust washed over Ivy as she took in the sight of it, but her curiosity was still piqued. To Mrs. Sloan, she asked, "May I?"

She looked at Ivy warily, then nodded. "If anyone else here knows magic, it would be you. Be careful with it."

Ivy picked it up. The folder's texture felt off and shifted under her fingertips, as if the thing was alive. She suppressed a shudder as she opened it to reveal sheets of yellowed foolscap. It took a few seconds for her to decipher the faded handwriting. She gently flipped through the pages, a little surprised that the spells appeared to be written in ordinary black ink and not blood. She made out a few unfamiliar incantations, written in Latin, all of which called on a dark fae entity. The words themselves were grandiose threats that bordered on parody. Had they been written in English, they would have been at home in the pages of a poorly written penny serial about a witch who boiled children alive. It wasn't the words that had her breath catching in her throat and a chill coursing through her veins, but the paper itself, the folder that felt like living skin. It was an evil thing that she had to resist throwing away from herself. Against all instincts, she set on the table next to the mismatched tea set. "Ugh."

"Horrible, isn't it? Every time I've tried to burn the damn thing, it comes back." Mrs. Sloan looked at it with contempt. "I trust both of you will keep it out of the hands of anyone who would actually want it."

"Why not return it to the fae?" Ivy asked.

"I'd rather not seek them out, and the seelie fae would want nothing to do with this or an unseelie descendant, even if we're living like normal people." She picked up her cup and took a healthy gulp of her tea that had to be cold by now. "I want that back in one piece. Well, I don't *want* it, I just want to keep it out of the hands of anyone who would use it."

"I don't think it would let itself stay in pieces if we destroyed it," Merritt said.

"Likely not. Are you sure you still want to take it?"

Ivy had spotted spells for the dead in there, although she hadn't wanted to hold the folder in her hand any longer than necessary, so she hadn't read them too carefully. "I suppose so."

"I want *you* back in one piece, too," Mrs. Sloan added, with a knowing look at Merritt. "And listen to me when I say to look for this necromancer fellow before trying out any of those spells. Dress up, make a night of it, and look for him at séances before you do something stupid."

"We will, and I promise I'll return this." Merritt promised. He picked up the folder between two fingers and tucked it under his arm. "Although I suspect if it was lost, it would find its way back here."

"It could also end up in the hands of someone who would unleash God knows what into the world," Mrs. Sloan replied. "Let me pack you a basket before you go."

"Thank you, but that won't be necessary."

"Yes, it is." Mrs. Sloan gave Merritt and Ivy a look that told them she was not to be trifled with.

Ivy couldn't help but hide her smile behind her hand.

Mrs. Sloan bustled about in the kitchen for a few minutes. Merritt stood and collected their coats, then tucked the spells' folder into a pocket. He cringed as he did so, and Ivy knew one didn't need to be capable of casting spells to feel the malevolence written on the papers inside. His mother returned a few minutes later with a basket covered with a linen cloth. "For supper," she said.

Merritt hugged her before taking it. "Thank you."

"It was nice to meet you, Mrs. Thaddeus."

"You, as well." She was eccentric and much more forward than Ivy was expecting. She still sensed warmth and kindness to Mrs. Sloan. She was someone who truly tried to be a good person, unseelie fae lineage be damned.

"I'm sure we'll see one another soon. I'll tell your father you stopped by." Mrs. Sloan said as she followed them to the front door. Before she closed it after them, she added, "Be safe out there. I mean it."

"Why wouldn't I be?"

Mrs. Sloan rolled her eyes. "Be careful and come back alive. If you don't, by all the gods in heaven and hell, I'll summon your ghost myself to yell at you."

# CHAPTER 9

Merritt mulled over the events at his parents' home, unsure if he was more embarrassed or amused by his mother's antics. He probably should have let her know ahead of time that he would be stopping by, and he certainly should have told Ivy what his parents were like.

The folder of spells in his coat pocket seemed to pulse against him. He resisted the urge to open the steam cab's dirty window and pitch it outside. Instead, he focused on the smell of the food in the basket on the seat next to him, mixed with the dusty odor of the cab and whatever floral perfume Ivy wore.

The cab left them outside Merritt's flat. The afternoon sun was setting, a reminder of the approaching winter. "Are you hungry?" he asked after he unlocked the house's front door. "We didn't have dinner."

"I haven't been able to stomach the thought of food since last night. I suppose I should eat something."

Claudia waited for them at the top of the stairs. "Where have you been?" she asked. "You are gone all night! I was getting worried."

"I had a case to tend to," Merritt replied as he unlocked his flat door. He left his coat and hat on hooks beside it, then took Ivy's coat.

"Is Claudia here?" Ivy asked.

"I'm always here." Claudia waited until the door was open before gliding into the flat. "I thought you were already employed on a case. You got drunk over it."

To Ivy, Merritt said, "Claudia's here and says hello." To the ghost, he said, "My getting drunk that night was an accident, and I was sacked from the case this morning. In a related twist, Mrs. Thaddeus's housekeeper was murdered last night." He regretted the flip words as soon as they left his mouth. The last thing he wanted to do was upset Ivy further.

"Did you speak to her?"

"I did, and she gave me a description of her killer. We're going to look for him." He unpacked the basket. To Ivy, he said, "My apologies. I've never had a visitor while Claudia's here. I didn't intend to be insensitive."

"You hardly ever have visitors at all," Claudia pointed out. She picked at an invisible piece of lint on her stola.

"I have one this evening for tea," Merritt explained as patiently as he could. He liked Claudia, odd as she was, but he hoped to have a little bit of time alone with Ivy. Their plan was to go out walking, see which hotels and clubs were holding séances that evening. If Roger McCann was a regular visitor to such ridiculous displays, it stood to reason that the medium he employed to trap Dr. Thaddeus would be easily available on the local circuit.

Claudia glanced at him, then at Ivy, who waited in the middle of the sitting room, looking aimlessly around the flat. "Oh." Understanding dawned on her face. "Merritt, I've never known you to fancy anyone before."

Merritt didn't reply. He silently thanked every deity he

could think of that Ivy couldn't read his mind or hear Claudia. He'd never voiced what he thought about Ivy and he wouldn't now, not when she was his client.

"She doesn't know," Claudia said patiently. "And you can't say anything while she's here."

Merritt set places at his small table before he unpacked the basket. "Can I get you something to drink?" he asked Ivy.

"A glass of water, please."

"No whiskey for either of you," Claudia said.

"Not tonight," Merritt replied. Catching Ivy's quizzical glance, he added, "That was to Claudia." He fetched two glasses of water from the kitchen sink. Part of the reason he'd wanted to rent the flat in the first place was because of its running water.

The ghost sighed dramatically. "Fine, I'll leave you to it. I can tell when I'm not wanted."

"You are. You're my friend. So is Ivy."

"So she's 'Ivy' now." Claudia tilted her head to the side, a knowing smile on her lips.

"Yes."

"I suppose if you're on a first name basis with Ivy, I should take my leave. If you're looking for me, I'll be in the flat across the corridor." Ivy glided away through the door.

Merritt pulled away one of the chairs at his tiny kitchen table and gestured for her to sit. "Claudia left."

Ivy sat and arranged her gray skirt around herself. "What did she say?"

Merritt sat opposite her and they each removed cold beef sandwiches from the basket in the middle of the table. He chose his words carefully. "She likes to hear about my goings-on outside. She's interested in this case." She was also extraordinarily perceptive. For half a second, he wondered if Ivy suspected anything about his unprofessional, inappropriate attraction to her. If Claudia could pick up on it, perhaps she could, too. He changed the subject. "Would you consider a trip to the factory tonight to look at McCann's office instead of a stroll? Minerva mentioned that the medium visited him there. There may be a calling card or something with his name on it."

"He usually works quite late," Ivy replied. "I recall Edwin mentioning that he'd stay late into the night, often past nine or ten o'clock."

"Why the hell would he do that? Factory owners don't work that late. They make their serfs do that."

"Edwin insisted on reasonable hours for the factory. The last shift works until seven and everything is shut down for the evening by seven-thirty. McCann once told me that he got his best work done at night."

That would make things a little more difficult, but not impossible. He recalled Minerva's words about McCann working late in the necromancer's presence. "He's usually left by nine, though?"

She nodded. "To my knowledge, yes."

"And he doesn't have any magical abilities? Would he be able to, I don't know, sense if someone has been in his office?"

"McCann doesn't have a shred of magic in him. I would have noticed it."

Merritt hesitated over his next question, unsure how it would be taken. "What about me?"

Was it his imagination, or did a blush color her cheeks? "You have a… well, glow, I suppose. Invisible to the naked eye." She stumbled a bit over the word *naked*. "I sensed something from you the moment we met, although I can't tell if it's from your necromancy skills or being part fae."

Ben and Elora Lang had mentioned that as well, prior to Merritt's revealing what he was. "I couldn't tell you which part of me causes that, either. Perhaps people with preternatural abilities have a way of recognizing each other that only we can sense, at least in the cases of the living."

"You've met dead people?" Just as quickly, she corrected herself. "You mentioned you know vampires."

"I'm acquainted with one and his human blood mate, yes." Merritt didn't have much in the way of friends, although he supposed Ben and Elora counted. "I'm not sure how to describe how vampires appear to me. I can sense the dead, of course, but there's something about vamps I can't put my finger on. 'Undead' really is the best way to describe them and their energy." Not quite alive, but not quite dead, either.

Ivy's curiosity was piqued. "What's a blood mate?"

"It's a blood exchange vampires and humans have when they want to stay with them for eternity. My vampire friend is also legally married to his. Of course, they couldn't do that in a church. I haven't asked for a lot of details as to the mate ritual." He suspected it was largely sexual in nature and if it wasn't, Ben and Elora definitely would make it so. There were certain details of his friend's lives that he didn't need to be informed of.

"How fascinating." She took a sip from her water glass. "I wish I'd had more of an opportunity to meet other people like us."

"I stopped consulting with the police because of people like us. I met my vampire friend when I investigated a murder that occurred near the house he was squatting in. Another vampire committed it."

"What happened to the vampire who did it?"

Merritt paused, choosing his next words carefully. The carnage that a vampire in the throes of bloodlust could wreak was unmatched with anything he'd seen from humans. The scenes he'd investigated still haunted him. "He's gone now. We made sure of that."

"We?"

He thought back to the gory scene that unfolded before him in an abandoned glassworks factory in London, nearly two years ago now. A shudder rippled through him as the memories of all the blood, the smells of rot, the torn apart bodies flooded back. "It was a joint effort. Me, Ben, and Elora." He hoped she didn't ask more questions about that incident, not wanting to think about that spring morning on the factory floor.

Ivy didn't prod further, and he wondered if she could sense his discomfort with the old memories. She rose and picked up their plates, now empty. "Let's get this cleaned up and we'll go to the factory."

She helped tidy the kitchen over Merritt's protests, and at half past eight they were back on the street. The temperature had dropped a couple of degrees, reminding him that winter was on its way. Envy flared through him when he thought about Ben and Elora, how they whiled away the colder weather in warmer climates. He wondered if they would stay in England at least for Christmas.

They took a steam cab to the Albert Dock, then walked the rest of the way, not wanting the vehicle to draw attention. The bottling factory's windows were dark, the doors locked when they arrived. Ivy murmured a spell in Latin, her eyes closed as she concentrated. Under the illumination offers by the gas lamps lining the street, she looked ethereal, like the magical being she was. She opened them a few seconds later. "The factory is empty."

Removing her gloves, she placed her hand on the wood and recited another spell. The heavy lock clunked and disengaged. Ivy pushed open the door, then motioned for Merritt to follow her.

He removed a flameless candle from his pocket and activated it, casting pale light on the foyer floor. Ivy recited another spell into her bare hand, causing flares of light to appear at her fingertips. Merritt couldn't keep himself from saying, "Wow."

She gave him a look over her shoulder that made his heart skip a beat.

His heart did so again when Minerva appeared in front of them, nearly bursting out of the wall. "What the fuck?"

Ivy shrieked, the sound echoing off the walls. "It's Minerva," Merritt said. The explanation did nothing to remove the rattled, wide-eyed look from Ivy's face. To the ghost, he said, "How are you?"

Minerva gave him a noncommittal shrug. "Still dead. You came at the right time. Roger McCann left not an hour ago."

"We won't be here long. We'll be taking a look at his office and leaving."

"Don't let us get in the way then. The sooner you get rid of that medium, the sooner we can breathe." She paused. "Well, not really. I'm certain you understand what I'm saying."

"I do. Please tell your friends I said hello."

Minerva nodded, her white wig's curls bobbing, before she melted through the wall she'd come from.

"My God," muttered Ivy. "You two nearly made my heart stop."

"She wants McCann exposed as much as we do."

Their conversation ceased as Ivy led him through the darkened factory, guided by the light offered by the flameless candle and her weirdly glowing hands. They took care on the stairs, pitch dark as the corridor was. Ivy cast her unlocking spell at Roger McCann's door and opened it with ease.

The room's window was covered by a drape. Ivy turned on a wall-mounted gas lamp, leaving the light low. Before them was the same impeccably arranged room Merritt stood in the last time he was here.

Both of them worked quickly, with Merritt carefully combing through the desk and Ivy the bookcase that held stacks of ledgers. The desk's contents were innocuous enough: lists of suppliers, contracts with vendors, nothing out of the ordinary for a patent medicine company. In one drawer, he found a black leather notebook too small to be a ledger. He carefully opened it to see a list of names and addresses, many of them crossed out. Monsieur Mist, Alice the All-Knowing, Mrs. Chesterton… "Ivy," he said urgently. "Take a look at this." She looked up from a ledger, her face ashen, and he forgot what he was about to say. "What's wrong?"

"This is a new formula," she whispered. "It's dated earlier this month. He wants to reformulate the Miracle Elixir and start production as early as the new year."

"Isn't that what you suspected he wanted to do?"

"Yes, but this is worse than I thought. This new formula would be nothing but laudanum with a little valerian added to it, perhaps some lavender. That's it." Quiet, controlled rage crept into her voice. "That isn't what Edwin wanted! That isn't what I want!" She looked as if she wanted to rip the book in half, but she put it back on the bookcase exactly where she found it. She looked at the notebook in Merritt's hands. "What's that?"

"A list of names that sound like charlatans." He flipped through the pages. "The only one that isn't crossed out is a Mr. Penright."

Ivy shook her head. "I've never heard of him."

"It could be the necromancer." He refrained from mentioning Martha's murder, not wanting to distress her further. He replaced the notebook in the desk drawer. "Penright. I haven't heard of him either, but I can make some enquiries." He sighed. "I may have to sit in on a séance."

Minerva glided through the wall. "Mr. McCann's at the door."

"Shit." He looked at Ivy. "Minerva's just informed me that McCann's here."

"What? Why?" She looked around the room, as if she'd forgotten where the exit was. Her panic was palpable in the air.

"Just hide in the drying room. He never goes up there," Minerva suggested.

"Where's the drying room?" Merritt whispered.

Ivy froze for a second, unsure what to do. Finally, she grabbed his arm, then dimmed the gas lamp. "At the end of the corridor. Come on."

On tiptoes, they crept along the dark corridor, Merritt praying that McCann couldn't hear them and that he hadn't brought his necromancer friend with him. Ivy stumbled over her spell as she unlocked the drying room door, nearly shoving Merritt inside before closing it behind her. She whispered another spell, probably one to keep it locked. Merritt didn't dare re-light his flameless candle.

Light from one of the lane's street lamps outside offered a little illumination. The room was cast in shadows, revealing rows of tables crowded with dried herbs. The pleasant scent of them hung in the air, sweet and earthy, reminding Merritt of the back garden at his parents' home. That memory was pushed aside as he and Ivy wordlessly stared at each other, Ivy's eyes wide with terror. He hated to see that look on her face.

Footsteps, sure and confident, strode down the corridor. Nervousness flared in Merritt.

Down the corridor came the sound of another door being opened on hinges that squeaked in protest, then silence. Merritt caught Ivy's gaze again, noting that she didn't look like she was ready to faint or be sick.

She gave a soft sigh and leaned against the wall before sliding to the floor in a tangle of gray and lavender skirts that she rearranged around her legs.

Merritt did the same. He hoped McCann, or whoever it was, didn't plan on spending all night in his office. He removed his notebook from his coat pocket and turned it to a fresh page. He pried out the small pencil stuck in the gap in the spine. By the light offered by the street, he scribbled, *Maybe he only forgot something.* He passed the notebook to Ivy, who peered at his looping scrawl before taking the pencil from him.

She hesitated before writing, *Is Minerva here?*

Merritt shook his head.

She nodded and set the notebook on her skirts. Ivy's hands moved in the darkness and her whispered incantation was so faint he could scarcely pick up the words. She stiffened for a few seconds before relaxing again against the wall, then picked up the notebook again and wrote, *he's alone.*

That was a relief to hear. All they had to do was wait out McCann's exit.

Half an hour passed in silence before Ivy's head tilted, softly landing on his shoulder. The contact startled him for half a second, before he noticed her breathing become deep and regular. She'd fallen asleep. Guilt threaded through him at the realization. Between the constant adrenaline that had been coursing through her over the last couple of days and the lack of rest, she was more exhausted than he thought. It had been foolish, suggesting a late night investigation when neither of them was sufficiently rested. Her head against him was a small gesture, but powerful. If he thought every sense of his was on high alert before, that awareness was nothing compared to the comfortable weight of her against his shoulder, the trust she'd placed in him to keep them safe. He didn't dare move, not wanting to disturb her nor wanting her to wake up startled. The smell of her hair reached his nose, a sweet smell not unlike the drying room's herbs.

From somewhere outside, bats screeched. Merritt shuddered and hoped that wasn't a sign of things to come.

He had nearly started to doze off himself when the same footsteps sounded down the corridor, this time away from the office. He didn't move, his ears straining to hear where McCann was headed. Taking care not to disturb Ivy, he fished his watch out of his pocket and held it so the exterior light could reach its face. It was nearly eleven. Was McCann finally gone?

As if she could read his mind, Minerva glided through the door, glowing in the darkness. "He's left," she reported. "You really must do something about him. We're getting tired of being disturbed during the night. This is our time."

Ivy stirred. "Mm?" He couldn't help but notice that the sound was adorable.

"Minerva's just told me that McCann's left for the evening." He rose and helped Ivy to her feet. To Minerva, he said, "Thank you. You wouldn't happen to know why he returned, would you?"

"You're very inquisitive, but that works in my favor. I followed him to his office. He did what he usually does in there at night, which is read over reports and write things down. There wasn't anything out of the ordinary, aside from him returning after he already left. He's only done that a couple of times. Perhaps he forgot something."

"Did he notice that we were in there? We looked through it and made sure not to leave a trace."

"He didn't appear to be alarmed, aside from having forgotten whatever he did. He sat at his desk, pulled out a few of his books, copied some words on a sheet of foolscap, and left with the copy." She shrugged and continued before Merritt could ask her to clarify. "I don't know what he copied. I died in 1745 and girls weren't encouraged to read the way they are now. I can't understand his handwriting style."

"That's all right." As he said the words, he realized they were true. As prickly as the ghost could be, Minerva had helped them a great deal when she didn't have to. "You've done a lot for this case the last few days. We really appreciate this."

"Is she back?" Ivy whispered.

"Can't your lady friend tell when you're speaking to a ghost? It's rather obvious," Minerva said.

There was that prickliness again. "This is all new to her," Merritt replied.

"Did you know that you look at her like you want to devour her?" Minerva fiddled with the jeweled necklaces that dangled nearly to where her navel would be beneath her layers of skirts and crinolines.

Why the hell was every ghost so perceptive about him these days? Claudia had said something similar. His answer was stiff. "I didn't."

"She looks at you that way, too. I don't think either of you can recognize it. It's actually sort of sweet."

His pulse sped up the mention of Ivy looking at him in that particular way and the base part of him wanted to ask Minerva about it further. It was as if he was ten years old again, infatuated with a neighborhood girl, desperate to know more about her and how she felt about him. A quick look at Ivy told him her current expression was one of confusion, not to mention it was rude to get into a lengthy conversation with a ghost when someone else present couldn't see or hear them. "I see."

"I don't care for the physical affections of men or women and never have. If I did, I would certainly find one or both of you sights for sore eyes." She adjusted one of her wig's curls and raised an eyebrow at the confused-looking Ivy. "All I ask is that you keep Mr. McCann's necromancer away from here. We don't bother anyone and we don't want to leave."

"I will do my best to see to that."

Her reply was sharp. "No. Don't try your best. Do your best. This is our home."

Merritt hesitated, desperately wanting to know why she and her friends insisted on spending eternity in a patent medicine bottling factory, but didn't. He'd always prided himself on being a polite necromancer who respected spirits' boundaries and emotions. He would continue to do so. He'd been sharing his floor with Claudia for the last six years and had managed to keep himself from asking her why she haunted the place. He suspected that she had forgotten after so many centuries. "I will," he promised.

"I will hold you to it." Her voice held a note of conviction that it hadn't before.

It left Merritt to wonder what kind of abilities she might have manifested since her death that she hadn't displayed to him yet. She melted through the wall, back to wherever she and her friends stayed. "She's gone," said Merritt.

"Care to enlighten me?" Ivy sounded irritated and tired.

He couldn't blame her. "Minerva said that McCann

came back to read over some numbers, as if he'd forgotten something. He left with one of the ledgers."

"He often takes paperwork home with him."

Merritt thought about the notebook with the necromancers' names, how he finally had one to go on. Penright. It was a start. Perhaps in the morning, he and Ivy…

She yawned, interrupting his thoughts.

Ivy was in no state to be traipsing around the city and wouldn't after at least one night of decent sleep. "Let me take you back to the hotel," he said. "You've been awake a long time."

"So have you." She unlocked the door and held it for him.

Even though the factory was now empty, both of them walked as quietly as they could, a force of habit for Merritt. "I don't need as much rest as you. I've done this kind of thing before." He activated his flameless candle. Ivy recited her light spell, making her fingers glow.

"You'll have to tell me about it sometime. What's the strangest thing you've waited for?"

He liked that she was talking, that she had relaxed a little. "In my spare time a couple of years ago, I surveilled an old warehouse. It was along the Albert Dock, actually. Thanks to some odd newspaper adverts from a quack scientist, I discovered experiments were being conducted on shapeshifters. I found evidence of a mermaid being held in the warehouse, but by then the scientist was found dead in a small village fifty or so miles from here."

"What of the mermaid?"

He noticed that she wasn't as surprised at the revelation of the existence of mermaids as she was about vampires. She must be getting used to the notion of other supernaturals. "I have my suspicions about what happened to the mermaid, all of which end in it escaping and staying alive. I think it may have killed the scientist, actually."

"Good." The vehemence in her voice struck something deep in him. "All of us want to just live out our lives, including mermaids. There are hardly any covens left in England because other people couldn't leave us be. Generations of knowledge and spells are gone forever. All thanks to hunts and burnings."

They had returned to the factory floor, still eerily quiet. A flash of ghostly activity caught his eye in the furthest corner of the room. Minerva and her friends looked up from their spectral teacups, their bright gowns and white wigs glowing in the darkness. Merritt waved goodbye.

The outside air was even colder now than it had been a couple of hours ago. Ivy's teeth chattered. "That was a fright," she muttered as they walked away.

Before he could offer it, she took his arm and clutched it like a lifeline. Minerva's words about how Ivy looked at him echoed in his mind. He reluctantly pushed them away. Even if it was true—and he suspected not, that his attraction was likely one-sided—she was his client. She had lost two people close to her in horrific ways and her stepson was out for her blood. The last thing either of them needed was that kind of complication.

# CHAPTER 10

It was nearly ten when Ivy woke the next morning, the latest she had slept in… how many years? She couldn't recall. Sunlight streamed through the hotel windows, a rarity for this time of year. The sight bolstered Ivy's spirits somewhat as she washed and dressed for the day, then sent for breakfast. It wasn't until she had her hat and coat on that she realized she had nowhere in particular to be. Guilt threaded through her. She'd nearly forgotten Martha and Edwin while she pretended life was normal for her and enjoyed the morning sun.

Merritt had walked her back to the hotel the night before and she had been too tired to coordinate their next meeting. At this time of day, he was bound to have left his flat for wherever he whiled away the day when he wasn't working on her case. Did he have any other cases, or had she monopolized his time enough? She had no idea. He did have an office close to the city center and that seemed the best place to find him. She left a message at the hotel's front desk in case he stopped by, then stepped outside into the crisp, sunny autumn morning.

Merritt's office was a short steam cab ride away in Nelson Street, and fifteen minutes later, she stood before a nondescript door in a rundown building. *Sloan Investigations* was painted on it in neat block letters. Ivy cast a short spell to see if anyone was inside before knocking. The incantation's magic immediately responded, Merritt's presence twanging through her. She smiled and knocked.

He opened the door immediately. He was hatless and coatless, as he was that first night she showed up at his flat. He was sober this time, and surprised. "Ivy."

Was it her imagination, or was there an affectionate note in his voice? She felt herself blush. "Good morning."

"Come in."

She let him take her coat, draping it over a peg on the wall next to another one that held his. She looked around the office, taking it in. It was spare, holding only a wooden desk with chairs on either side of it. A sad-looking maidenhair fern wilted in a pot in the corner.

"What brings you here this morning?" he asked. "I would have expected you to sleep some more."

"I've had enough. I feel better than I have in weeks." At least she did physically. She wouldn't start to feel right again in every other way until Edwin's soul was released from wherever it was, until Martha's murder had been avenged.

"I'm glad to hear it." He took a seat behind the desk and pushed a piece of paper across it.

She sat opposite him and picked it up. An address was written on it.

"I found out that Mr. Penright is holding a séance later tonight, open to members of the public. It's to be hosted by the Liverpool Museum of the Paranormal." A note of contempt had fallen into his voice as he said the name of the group.

"And we shall attend this séance?"

"I've been considering this and how to proceed. It's to be held in an auditorium, so there won't be any sitting around a table, holding hands and chanting nonsense. Presumably, the auditorium will be dark to add to the theatrics. If we sit in the back and don't draw attention to ourselves, Mr. Penright may not notice us at all."

It was a workable plan, and yet… "Mr. Penright was sent to kill me. He'll know what I look like." Merritt opened his mouth to reply, but she continued. "I don't care. He's trapped Edwin and he killed Martha. I'll go anyway."

Merritt froze for a few seconds, gathering himself. "Are you certain?"

She nodded, fury rising in her. "Yes. I'll disguise myself. He would be looking out for a woman in widow's weeds, if he was looking for me at all." Despite the gravity of the situation, the possibility of wearing something other than black or gray was thrilling, a tiny bit of fun that broke up the depressing, sad months of her mourning period. "I'll buy a new gown for this evening, rearrange my hair into a more youthful style. I'll do my best not to look like an old widow. I'm sure I can manage pulling that off for one evening."

"You aren't old at all."

Ivy looked at him in surprise. She hadn't been expecting that. "I'm older than you."

"I'm not old, either."

"I'm nearly forty." She couldn't believe she was saying this, discussing her age with the man originally hired to investigate her for murder, but here she was. For some strange reason, it felt imperative to tell him that, as if she wanted him to make an informed decision about… what? What could he possibly have to decide about her? They were client and employer, nothing more, as much as her stupid body wished it could be different. Their age difference was far smaller than the one she shared with Edwin, besides.

"Thirty-eight is hardly forty, and in the grand scheme of things isn't that far off from thirty-one. Neither of us are long in the tooth."

She nearly asked him how he knew her age, before she remembered Ezra. Her stepson would have handed over every scrap of information he had about his despised stepmother. It was flattering to hear that he remembered that part of her, that it didn't bother him. In the grand scheme of things, how had he considered their age difference in the context to their relationship? She wasn't sure it would be appropriate to dwell on that. She changed the subject. "Have you been to a séance of this size in an auditorium before?" Was it her imagination, or did disappointment flicker across his features at the change in subject? Just as quickly, it was gone.

"Unfortunately, when the spiritualism craze started. My parents brought me and my sister to one and had a family evening of making fun of the mediums. We went out for supper afterward. We still joke about it."

Ivy could already picture Mrs. Sloan's running commentary during such an event. She smiled. "Is the plan to attend and see if he matches the description Martha gave us of her killer?"

"Yes, and to see if there are any spirits there he's actually summoned of his own power. If any are trapped, I'll have to find a way to free them."

Ivy's breath caught. "Do you suppose it's possible he's kept Edwin's soul? I never thought to ask that. Can necromancers keep souls to do whatever they want them to do? I can't imagine going there tonight to find out that he's performing for a crowd at Penright's command like a puppet!"

"It's possible. I don't know how he would do it," Merritt replied. His voice was gentle. "We'll slip in, watch for long enough to see if he's tall and silver-haired, see the extent of his abilities. We'll be disguised as best as we can be and slip out before the séance ends. No one will notice us."

"All right." She tried to tamp down the sick feeling that rose in her throat like bile when she thought about spirits being trapped for Penright's whims. "I trust you."

Something shifted in his expression at the words. "Thank you."

"What is the etiquette surrounding a séance?" she asked.

He sighed more dramatically than she'd ever heard from him before. She bit back a smile. "It's utterly ridiculous."

MERRITT DIDN'T CARE for pageantry, which was always the order of the evening when a séance was happening. As he strode through the Adelphi Hotel's doors that evening, clad in his only evening clothes, he thought about how he'd certainly endured worse methods of investigating over the course of his career. At least he would have Ivy on his arm for the night. That as a thought that would never cease to set his mind at ease.

He almost didn't recognize her when she walked—-no, *sailed*—into the Adelphi's lobby. He could've sworn all conversation ceased for a moment as she made her entrance. His heart stopped for a few beats as he took her in, a vision in a deep green dress the color of jade and matching fur cape. The color matched her eyes almost perfectly. Her dark hair was unbound, arranged in curls that cascaded over her shoulders and down her back. A green hat with a net half-veil was pinned to it that gave her a slightly mysterious air.

"How did I do with my disguise?" she asked breathlessly, hardly able to suppress her grin.

It took a moment for him to find his voice. "You look beautiful." He couldn't help the words. He wasn't sure he wanted to. They were true. Something flickered across her features that he couldn't identify.

"But do I look like *me*? Would Mr. Penright recognize me if he saw me in the back of an auditorium?"

Once again, it took a few seconds for her words to register. "No." He might notice her for other reasons, the same ones that every man in the lobby right now did. "Where did you find this?"

"I rented it from a shop the hotel recommended. It was either this or a pink and gold ball gown," she said. She looped her hand through his arm and let him guide her out of the hotel. "I would've liked to wear the ball gown. I miss wearing colors."

"Colors suit you." They walked into the cool night air and he whistled for a passing cab to stop. It rolled to a halt at the curb, steam issuing from its vents.

"Speaking of suits, it's nice to see you in one."

He'd be damned if that compliment didn't make him want to lift the veil away from her face to kiss her. Instead, he gave her hand an affectionate squeeze as he helped her into the cab's seat before climbing in next to her.

The cab left them at a new-looking building in Bold Street whose painted door sign announced it to be the Liverpool Museum of the Paranormal. A few people were letting themselves into the building, taking no notice of

Merritt and Ivy. He hoped his contempt for it didn't show on his face.

Evidently, it did. "You look like you want to kick it," murmured Ivy as she adjusted her cape around her shoulders.

"I sort of do." The building was too ostentatious for his taste, its green glass windows flanked by small gargoyles on either side. The top of the building was lined with electric lights that flickered and popped as he watched them. It was an effect of poor wiring and not a mischievous spirit. A giant poster was nailed to the wall beside the door advertising a seance held by the Amazing Penright. To Merritt's disappointment, the poster didn't have an illustration of Penright. It would have saved them time and his sanity.

"The sooner we go in there, the sooner we can leave," Ivy pointed out. "And the sooner we can find out how to free Edwin's spirit."

Ah, yes. The late Dr. Thaddeus, the whole reason he was here with his wife this evening. His wife, who looked like a dessert in her evening wear and had over the course of his knowing her he hadn't been able to stop thinking about. He felt like a cad. "Of course." He guided her into the building and his nostrils flared at the odor. He suppressed a sneeze, but barely. How much incense was Penright burning, exactly? To add insult to injury, a black-suited employee told him that night's admission was five pence. Merritt gritted his teeth and paid for him and Ivy.

The foyer was well-lit by a combination of electric lights and candles. The crowd was bigger than Merritt expected, and he guessed there had to be at least forty or fifty people filling the auditorium. The walls and ceiling were draped with swaths of black cloth that looked like the kind used for mourning clothes, with flickering electric light sconces installed between pieces. Black fabric was draped over each of the chairs, lined in rows along the floor. At the opposite end of the auditorium was a dais that rose about a foot off the polished floor. It was empty save for a table draped in purple cloth, a pair of fat black candles on top of it, unlit.

There was not a ghost to be found around the place. Merritt bit back a smile before he remembered why he was here. "This is a good spot," he murmured to Ivy, pointing to a pair of seats in the second to last row. They were close to the door and the electric light didn't quite reach it. Between the dim illumination and Ivy's disguise, Merritt was fairly certain they would go unnoticed. Well, not entirely unnoticed. He sneaked a glance at Ivy. She did look amazing, after all.

A few moments after they took their seats, the lights dimmed and a rush fell over the crowd. It looked like nearly every seat in the auditorium was filled. A light glowed from somewhere behind the dais before a robed figure stepped on to it to a light smattering of applause. The face was hidden behind a hood.

Hadn't Martha said she was killed by a man wearing a robe with a hood? Hadn't Minerva mentioned a man who wore one, too? Heart hammering against his ribs, Merritt leaned forward in anticipation.

The figure raised his arms to silence the crowd, then lowered the hood. The lights turned back up. The face of a man who looked to be in his mid-forties appeared, his close-cropped hair shining silver in the lamplight.

Even though Merritt had been expecting to see a silver-haired man on the dais, it still shook him. He'd stared at the countenances of dozens of killers and doing so never failed to shake him. There was something different about this man, a different shade of evil. He sneaked a glance at Ivy, whose hands were fisted in her skirt's fabric. Her lips were thinned in anger as she stared at Penright.

"He keeps ignoring me, the bastard."

He closed his eyes briefly before acknowledging the ghost standing next to him. He didn't respond. Where had the ghost slunk in from?

"You're going to ignore me, too, is that it?" The ghost was a man wearing clothing far finer than Merritt had ever been able to afford. His clockwork eye whirred, causing Merritt to wonder why he'd kept it in his ghostly form. "My worthless nephew has my dukedom."

Merritt sighed and hoped the ghost didn't notice.

"His sister's married to a demon. Elora was always an opportunistic little tart."

He tried not to show his surprise at hearing the name. It was a smaller world than Merritt thought it could be. He kept his expression impassive as he waited for Penright to do something on the dais. Elora Lang's uncle had been a duke, and after he'd died in the wilds of Scotland, the dukedom had gone to his only heir, Elora's older brother.

"The hell with you," the ghost snarled.

On the dais, Penright's eyes were squeezed shut and he started to chant. The words were nonsense, utter gibberish, but the audience seemed to love it. Finally, in English, he proclaimed, "Any spirits present here this evening, show yourselves!"

"I've been here all along, you arsehole!" The ghost appeared next to Penright on the dais, but the medium didn't react. "My wastrel nephew is throwing away every-thing I've ever owned and you won't do anything about it!"

Penright opened his eyes and looked around the audi-torium, as if seeing it for the first time. "My God," he said in wonder. "So many spirits here tonight. You, there." He gestured at empty air and tilted his head to the side, like he was listening. "Yes. I see." To the crowd, he said, "Is there anyone here called… Potter, is it? Or Potman?"

"My sister-in-law was Mrs. Potter." A woman in the front row rose, her all-black attire swallowing her in the dim light. She turned to face the audience. "She passed one year ago today."

Sympathetic murmurs raced through the auditorium. Merritt couldn't believe what he was seeing. The scam was more blatant than he expected and he was appalled people were eating it up like candy.

"What is she saying?" the woman wailed dramatically. Any second now she would start weeping.

Penright put a hand on his forehead, as if in concentration. "She says it's all right. Everything is all right. She forgives you."

"Fuck this," the ghost said.

Merritt silently agreed.

"Your sister-in-law says that it doesn't matter anymore where she is," Penright continued. His eyelids fluttered. "She says goodbye and she gives you her blessing."

The woman let out an indistinguishable cry before sitting down, sobbing.

Now that the stage was set for more trickery, Penright opened his eyes and stared out at the crowd. "There are so many spirits here that I can't listen to them all."

"There's one and you won't fucking listen to him!" the ghost shouted. He floated to the dais with more speed than Merritt thought possible, then kicked a ghostly leg at the medium. Penright flinched but didn't react otherwise.

"Another woman stood up. Her voice trembled. "My daughter. Is she here?"

Somehow, Merritt doubted this was part of the grift, unlike the other melodramatic patron. His heart squeezed.

He knew the haunted look, the catching voice of a bereaved parent.

"What is your daughter's name? There are a lot of them here tonight," Penright said.

He might be a true necromancer, but he was a piss-poor showman. He couldn't even cold read properly as far as Merritt could tell.

"Violet," the woman replied.

"Violet what?"

"Violet Smith."

"Mrs. Smith, do you have something that belonged to your daughter that I may meditate on?"

Merritt's breath caught at the request, certainly an unusual one for a grifter.

Mrs. Smith hurried to the dais and handed a knitted blue scarf to the necromancer. Penright accepted it and murmured a few words over it in a language he couldn't understand. A few seconds later, an image of a young girl, perhaps fourteen or fifteen, appeared. She blinked in confusion before gasping in shock at the sight of her mother. "Why am I here?" she yelped.

"Mrs. Smith, your daughter is with us," Penright announced, the first honest thing he said all evening. "What do you have to ask her?"

Mrs. Smith let out a sob. "Tell her I miss her and I love her so much."

Violet's ghost burst into tears. "I miss her, too." She floated across the dais to her mother and tried to hug her, but her arms went through her. Mrs. Smith didn't appear to notice. She turned to Penright. "Why can't I touch her? Why did you force me here just to make me see her crying?"

Merritt's heart broke for both of them.

Penright muttered something else, a spell, Merritt

guessed. He thought about the fae spells his mother gave him and wondered if it was one of them. "I'm with Papa," Violet said suddenly, as if the thought had just struck her. "We're on the spirit plane together. We play cards every day."

"Mrs. Smith, did Violet enjoy playing cards with a man in her life. Her father or grandfather, perhaps? She mentioned her papa."

The weeping mother nodded. "Her father passed three years ago. They played Russian Bank together. He taught her when she was little."

"He made me say that!" Violet cried. She whipped her head in Penright's direction. "Send me back right now! Why are you doing this to my mama?"

"She and her papa play Russian Bank together. They're happy and safe on the other side." Penright gave the crowd a beatific smile while Violet raced to the dais and tried to snatch her scarf out of his hands. She wept in frustration when she couldn't.

The duke's ghost was watching all of this unfold, his mouth set in a straight line. "He's a piece of dogshit," he said. Violet looked up at him as if seeing him for the first time. She shrank back a little at the sight of the other ghost's clockwork eye.

Mrs. Smith reached up to take Penright's hand. "Thank you," she said, her voice catching. "I need to know that she's safe where she is. Please tell her I'm sorry."

"For what, Mama?" Violet cried. She wiped away tears that sparkled in the light. "I had pneumonia. It wasn't your fault! I'm not angry with you, I never was!"

"She says she understands," Penright replied.

"No, I'm telling her I'm not upset! Papa and I miss her so much! Why did you bring me here to torture me?" Violet reached out to her mother as Penright returned the scarf to her. The girl slowly faded away before she could speak again.

Merritt was horrified, a feeling that only intensified when Mrs. Smith placed coins in Penright's palm. The necromancer quickly spirited them away in a pocket of his voluminous robe.

"My God," Merritt whispered under his breath.

"What is it?" Ivy asked. "What the hell am I seeing?"

"Less than what I've seen. I'll tell you later." He tried to think about how the scene before them would have looked to someone who couldn't see the dead, and concluded that it would have been confusing at best, fake at worst.

An elderly man stood up. "Is my Eva here?"

Merritt suppressed a frustrated sigh. It was going to be a long evening of deception and fraud.

Ivy didn't know what she hated most about this evening: Merritt's obvious horror and discomfort at what was happening around them, or Penright's obvious fleecing of the audience. Some of the people asking questions were obvious plants, like the first woman who all but threw herself at Penright's feet asking her late sister-in-law for forgiveness. Ivy wondered what she'd allegedly done. Had she stolen money or carried on an affair with the dead woman's husband? Wouldn't that make the sister in law's husband the woman's brother? She shuddered.

The presentation lasted for hours.

Ivy's feet were asleep when the lights were finally turned up and Penright announced that he could be booked for private séances. A few people lingered around the dais to ask for details, but Merritt immediately guided her to the auditorium's doors. "What do you think?" she whispered to him.

"I think I've managed to discover the first genuine medium who is also a fraud," he replied.

His breath ruffled her hair, making her skin tingle, a feeling she hadn't expected to have during such an occasion. She recalled the stunned look on his face in the hotel lobby, when he saw her out of mourning, her hair out of its sensible knot, for the first time. She'd felt the same way then with his eyes on her. She forced the feeling away, concentrating on the more urgent matters at hand as they walked out of the building and into the chilly night. She pulled her fur cape a little more securely around herself. Idling steam cabs lined the side of the street. They walked along it as the cabs were hailed, looking for an available vehicle. It would be a bit of a wait, based on how many people ran for the cabs as soon as they left the museum. "Did he actually summon anyone?" she asked.

They walked under a street lamp, casting shadows over his face in a way she thought was symbolic. "A few times. The spirits weren't expecting to be put through that. It's all an elaborate ruse for money. It's cruelty for the sake of cruelty. He knows what's doing."

"So he's a real necromancer?" She kept her voice low, mindful of the people around them.

"He's a necromancer practicing dark magic, pretending to be a charlatan. There was a ghost who wasn't summoned by him and was just haunting the area. He noticed me and cursed me a few times when I didn't respond to him."

"Oh, no."

"It's a smaller world than I thought, because I suspect that the uninvited ghost is the uncle of the vampire's wife

I'm acquainted with. Of course, I wasn't in a position to ask him about that."

"Do you think you'll ever get a chance to…" Ivy's words died in her throat as she took in the sight ahead of her. Roger McCann, arguing with a steam cab driver about fares, not ten feet away from them. She froze and turned to Merritt, any faith in her disguise evaporated. Merritt looked equally surprised to see the man and lowered his head, obscuring his face with his hat brim.

McCann's head turned in their direction. Without ceasing in his beratement of the driver, he flinched, then squinted in their direction. The driver yelled at him in response, and McCann's attention was turned back to him.

Merritt grabbed her elbow and whirled both of them in the opposite direction, toward the museum. Nausea roiled through her as their paces picked up to a brisk walk and she hoped she didn't stumble. She didn't dare look back.

"Do I know you?" McCann called. At least he sounded genuinely curious.

They didn't answer, just kept walking. Merritt wrapped his arm around her waist, pulling her closer. A flutter that had nothing to do with the danger at hand raced through her at the contact. She did likewise, snaking her arm around him, hoping to throw off McCann. Merritt pressed his lips against her hair in a mock kiss, then whispered, "Turn left."

She shouldn't be as affected as she was by all of this, shouldn't be thinking about how much she wished they weren't being tailed by the man who had something to do with her husband's death…

He turned into a lane between two buildings, devoid of light save for a single gas lamp affixed to the side of one of them. Lights beckoned on the other end of the lane, along with a few people strolling the street. Could they be rid of McCann that easily?

"Hello?" McCann called out again. Ivy's heart sank. It would appear not.

"Damn it," Merritt muttered.

Ivy paused, then grabbed his coat's lapels and pulled him to her. The motion knocked his hat askew and she grabbed his hand, keeping him from adjusting it. "Pretend to kiss me," she whispered.

He looked confused for half a second, then leaned closer to her, pressing his body against hers. His free hand wrapped around her waist, hers around his neck, his face leaned closer, lips hovering above her mouth. His eyes fastened on hers, and she thought she could see a question reflected there. Or perhaps it was her own need to kiss him.

She leaned into him, lightly grazing her lips against his. His breath stuttered. Time seemed to stand still, and she wondered for a brief, awful moment if she hadn't made everything awkward.

He leaned in for a deeper kiss, one that was almost lazy, as if he had all the time in the world to explore her mouth. Her skin prickled, her knees went weak, and she was suddenly grateful for the wall at her back and his arms around her to keep from collapsing to the cobbles. He kissed with a confidence that he knew he would get to do it again.

"Have we met?"

McCann's voice had all the effect of having a bucket of cold water being thrown on them.

With a frustrated sigh, Merritt pulled his hat away from his face just enough so he could snarl, "No. We've never met. And you're interrupting us." There was real vitriol in his voice.

Ivy closed her eyes, praying McCann wouldn't recognize her. She held her breath, waiting for him to ask what the hell she was doing but all that happened was McCann's affronted reply. "Begging your forgiveness."

"Fuck off," snapped Merritt.

McCann's footsteps tapped along the lane, away from them.

"Do you think," Ivy began, but Merritt cut her off when he kissed her again. She forgot what she was going to say as she eagerly kissed him back. His hat fell to the ground, unnoticed, as he gripped her hips against him. Even through her myriad layers of skirts she could feel the hard proof of his arousal, a sensation that had every cell in her body begging for more. Her clothes felt unbearably tight, too constricting against her skin as Merritt kept kissing her. She felt a distinct chill when he pulled away from her and fetched his hat.

"I should get you back to your hotel." His voice was rough.

She thought she detected a note of reluctance there.

She remembered when she was going to ask him. "Do you think McCann recognized us after all?"

Merritt thought about it for a few seconds. "No. You're a widow still in mourning. He would have said something."

His reminder of what she was, how she was still viewed in society as nothing more than an ornament to be hidden away now that her husband was dead, stung. She didn't imagine hearing that from someone she had kissed so passionately, who had returned her affections with equal enthusiasm, would hurt as much as they did.

Merritt Sloan had just come to his senses, and he was mortified.

She swallowed the lump in her throat before speaking. "Yes. I'd like to return to the hotel."

# CHAPTER 11

Spending the morning at his rented office felt rather pointless, but Merritt couldn't think of any other place that would offer him the quiet he needed to think. If he stayed any longer at his flat, Claudia would notice something was amiss with him and demand answers, and he didn't dare bother Ivy at her hotel.

He'd behaved abominably last night. He couldn't believe how badly he had fucked up. Merritt had never been physical with any of his clients, nor had he ever mentally entertained such a liaison. He'd always prided himself on professionalism. Yet the second Ivy's survival instincts kicked in—and he had to admit her method of ridding themselves of McCann was a good one—any sense of professionalism disappeared. He'd been glad to kiss her, would have done more if the opportunity presented itself. What was worse was he would do it again if Ivy wanted it.

So, he whiled away the morning in his office, making notes about Penright's performance and trying to reconcile the spells he chanted with the ones his mother loaned him. He could hardly make heads of tails of the words, scribbled from memory, a phonetic mess. Ivy might be able to help, but he didn't want to impose further.

He had boiled a second pot of tea and sat down to drink a cup when a knock sounded at his door. His heart leapt. "Ivy?" His voice was quiet and hesitant, more of a wish than acknowledging who could be on the other side.

Another knock at the door in response. Merritt opened it, then started in surprise. "Elora?"

The vampire's wife stood before him, resplendent in a bright blue dress and matching jacket. "Good morning."

"Come in." He stepped aside to let her pass. "Tea?"

"Please." She sat down in the chair across from his desk.

"What brings you here? I didn't think you and Ben would have any reason to visit Liverpool."

"Our ship departs from Albert Dock in three days' time. I've been running around during the day, making sure we'll be able to get light-tight accommodations aboard. It was the only one we could find that has a late night departure." She unpinned her hat and set it on her lap. "I thought I'd stop by and see how you're doing before we go to Spain."

A flare of jealousy sparked in him at the mention of their travels. Being from a family of industry, Ben had access to funds that Merritt could only dream of. Their lives, or unlife, as was Ben's situation, were spent traveling and taking in nighttime sights. Probably more than that in private, if the faded puncture marks on Elora's neck was any indication, but Merritt didn't need to be privy to those details. "It's good to see you," he said. "Actually, this is quite the coincidence. You aren't going to believe who spoke to me last night."

Her eyes widened in alarm. "Vampires aren't on killing sprees around Liverpool, are they? Ben and I would help with that, of course, although he'll be quite cross at having to reschedule our departure."

"No, nothing like that. Your uncle was the Duke of Wexfield, was he not?"

Her expression darkened. "He died in an accident in Scotland."

"He did, and I have no idea why his ghost would be haunting a paranormal museum in Liverpool, but he is."

"What?"

"I had to attend a, well, 'séance' isn't the correct word. It was a ridiculous performance designed to upset summoned spirits and fleece their survivors of their funds. Your uncle's ghost was present and demanded an audience with a necromancer."

"And you're the necromancer?" Confusion crossed her features, and Merritt sighed. He would have to backtrack a bit.

He told her about his investigation, Martha's murder, how Dr. Thaddeus's spirit was being held in limbo, what little he knew about Penright. Elora looked more surprised and intrigued with each new piece of information. Merritt told her everything, except for the part about kissing Ivy in the lane.

"Hm." Elora leaned back in her seat and took a few thoughtful sips of her tea.

"Hm, what?"

"After what Ben and I have experienced at the hands of vampires, I really shouldn't be surprised at how the dead misbehave, but here we are." She drained her cup and set it on the desktop. "So, this young Mr. Thaddeus sacked you?"

"Yes."

"Yet you're still investigating this case."

"Ivy rehired me."

"She's 'Ivy,' then." Elora gave him a knowing look.

Irritation flared in Merritt at the knowledge that yet another person had noticed his fondness for Ivy. "Yes, we've become friends. She's important to me. Ensuring the dead can move on to the next plane is also important to me."

Elora gave him a look he couldn't decipher, as if she knew something he didn't. She didn't elaborate on Ivy. "Don't worry about Uncle Frederick. He deserves to wander the earth for the rest of time."

He was grateful for the change in subject. "Why would your uncle be haunting a building in Liverpool? I thought your family was from London."

"It is, but Uncle Frederick owned property in other parts of England, including a few buildings in Liverpool that aren't entailed. Where exactly was this séance held?"

"At a recently converted museum in Bold Street."

She nodded. "Ah. He owned one there that my brother must have sold off, although I can't recall the exact address. Oh, well. Serves him right for turning me out when I was an orphaned child."

Her brother had done the same when he inherited the dukedom. Merritt couldn't summon any sympathy for the late duke, either.

Elora steered the conversation back to his case. "So, how are you going to defeat this Penright fellow and release Dr. Thaddeus' soul?"

"I'm still working on that. I suspect he's involved in dark magic, so I'll need Ivy's help with the spell work. I can't cast."

"But Penright can? You're both necromancers."

Merritt shrugged. "I don't know what else he is. Perhaps there's a witch in his lineage, or his fae heritage is stronger than mine. I can commune with the dead and only commune with the dead."

"You say that as if it's a common skill. Can't you raise the dead?" She helped herself to more tea.

"Of course it isn't. I'm just stymied by this case. I've never had one like this before, and I hate that I can't get to the bottom of it as quickly as I want." He shifted, uncomfortable at the direction the conversation had taken. "I haven't been able to raise anything from the dead since I was a child, and that was an accident." Seeing her eyes widen, he added, "It was only recently deceased animals." That wasn't entirely true, but he didn't want to discuss what else he had done before he could control his power.

"Did you bring the roast chicken on the supper table back to life?"

He smiled. "No, but there was a rabbit my dog hunted." Just as quickly, his smile faded and a shudder rippled through him. Twenty-six years later, the memory still haunted him, almost as much as that of his grandfather's passing and what happened after.

"Could you just kill Penright? Would that release Dr. Thaddeus's trapped spirit?"

Merritt stared at her, agog. It was the second time someone had suggested that, and he was just as shocked as when his mother did.

"What's that look for? You and I both know that sometimes the only solution to a problem is to kill the cause of it. It sounds like the world would be better off without Penright in it." She tasted her tea and made a face. "It's gone cold."

"It's still drinkable."

"You didn't answer my question. Would killing him release souls he's trapped?"

"I don't know. Possibly. I'd rather free souls first before killing Penright, just to be on the safe side."

"Suit yourself. Which hotel is Mrs. Thaddeus staying at?"

Merritt raised his eyebrow in suspicion. "Why?"

"So Ben can feed from her."

The very notion of Elora's husband sinking his fangs into Ivy had Merritt's hackles on edge. Jealousy rose in him, fiery as erupting lava.

"You should see the look on your face right now. Of course, Ben wouldn't feed from anyone but me. It would be nice to meet her, is all."

Merritt sighed, feeling idiotic. "The Adelphi."

"That's perfect! We have a suite there until we depart. Let's have a drink together, shall we say at nine? We would love to meet her."

"You want to see if she meets your approval," Merritt translated.

"Well, yes. We'll want to make sure whoever has you tied up in knots is a nice person."

"She doesn't—you know, I'm not going to argue with you on this."

"Because there's no point." Elora gave him a smug smile over the rim of her cup.

"Ivy and I have more investigating to do tonight."

"That's why I suggested only having a drink. What room is she in? I can take her a note."

"No. I'll mention it to her myself." He rose and gathered his notes. "I'll head there now."

"We can share a cab." Before he could protest, she added, "Let me take you there. I'm paying the fare."

Her voice brooked no argument. Merritt put on his hat and coat, and followed her out of his office.

~

IT WAS NEARLY NOON, but Ivy hadn't bothered to dress yet. She sipped hot chocolate the hotel's staff brought to her and nibbled a biscuit. It was a poor excuse for a late breakfast, but she didn't care. She couldn't stop thinking about the kisses she'd shared with Merritt the night before, nor the awkward journey back to the hotel. Neither of them had spoken in the cab ride, and he'd bade her good night in the most perfunctory manner, as if he was her uncle and her a distant niece.

It hurt.

When was the last time she'd ever felt passion for another person? Certainly sometime before her marriage, if ever. She was nearing forty and had missed out on so much. "Don't think about that," she murmured to herself. "You made your choice when you and Edwin entered a marriage of convenience. It wasn't bad at all." It truly wasn't. She and Edwin had been best friends. What their marriage lacked in passion made up for in friendship and respect. She wished she could have the chance to have had *all* those things, as Edwin had with his first wife. She poured another cup of chocolate from its pot, noting that it had cooled. She cast a spell to reheat it when a knock sounded at the door.

Ivy wasn't expecting anyone. Perhaps it was the hotel staff. Crossing the room, she called, "Hello?"

"It's me," Merritt said from the other side.

A strange mixture of relief, excitement, and cautious swept through her when she opened the door. His eyes widened when he saw she was still in her nightgown and wrapper. "Come in," she said.

He didn't protest, instead walking into the room and shaking off his coat. He left it and his hat on the tree near the highboy, removing a leather-bound folder from the coat's pocket before he did so.

"What brings you here?"

"Friends of mine are staying here, and one of them stopped by for a visit," he explained. "Should I come back at a later time?"

She bit back a wry smile. Some of her anxiety about the night before dissipated. He was being polite. If he'd been bothered by the sight of her in her nightwear he would have left already. "Only if you want to."

"I don't." He tossed the folder on the unmade bed.

Ivy nodded at the folder. "What's that?"

"Notes from last night and my mother's spells. I hoped you could decipher some of the words Penright used last night."

"They were gibberish, as far as I could tell, but I'm not so familiar with dark magic. I can try." She reached for the folder and opened it. Barely legible scribbles that spelled incoherent words greeted her, along with sheets of yellowed foolscap with Mrs. Sloan's unseelie spells. The latter was a combination of old English dialects and Latin, nothing that was outside her abilities. She didn't dare say them out loud, not until she had a better idea of what the spells could do.

"What do you think?" Merritt asked.

"I'm going to have to return to my house at some point to look in my grimoires. I'd prefer not to try them out without researching them first." She closed the folder and set it aside on the table next to her chocolate pot and biscuits. At the sight of them, she remembered her manners. "May I offer you something to eat or drink?"

"No, thank you." He looked away for a moment, the tips of his ears pink. She steeled herself, knowing what was coming next. "About last night…"

"It was my fault," she blurted. "I took liberties. I panicked and didn't know what else to do."

He stared at her, aghast. "I beg your pardon?"

"I didn't know what else to do. I've never been, well, *hunted* before." She tried to lighten the mood with a joke. "It doesn't happen to witches that often these days."

He didn't smile. Her heart sank. "I've never been in that kind of situation before, either."

"I refuse to believe no one has ever chased you in your line of work."

"It's happened plenty of times, but I was almost always alone." He took a step closer to her.

Ivy's heart picked up its tempo, fluttering against her ribcage like a trapped bird. He tucked a strand of hair behind her ear, then lightly ran the backs of his fingers against her cheek. The small touch was electrifying, and it was all she could do not to throw herself into his arms.

"You improvised." His voice was soft. "You did very well and threw off McCann. I'm proud of you." His fingers trailed down her face to her exposed collarbone.

Ivy couldn't keep a small moan from escaping her at the contact. When she looked at Merritt, she saw his pupils had dilated in a way that wasn't entirely human. "The first time I saw you, I thought you might be an incubus," she confessed.

He clearly hadn't been expecting that. "What?"

She felt herself blush. "There's something, well, *otherworldly* about you, something intense. Sensual." She knew now it was his fae lineage.

He paused for a few seconds before a slow smile spread across his face. "*Oh.*"

That was an encouraging sign. Emboldened, Ivy said, "You kiss very well, too."

That earned another thoughtful look from him. "Perhaps it was the company." He took another step forward. "You think quickly on your feet."

Ivy nearly blurted out that she'd frozen in place while in the lane. She'd been unsure whether to run away and rouse McCann's suspicion or stay put and fight. She resisted, instead replying, "If being a witch ever becomes boring, I know I'll have other vocations available."

"You'd be a fine detective. All you have to do is cast a spell to find someone. It worked on me." He smiled, and something in her flip-flopped at the sight.

Her skin prickled with awareness, with the need to touch this man again without being impeded by layers of clothing. She was very conscious that she wore only a thin nightgown, and she'd caught Merritt's gaze traveling her form a couple of times since he'd arrived. Ivy took another step closer to him, encouraged. She reached out to touch his face with the pads of her fingers, thumb gently sweeping the corner of his mouth. He lightly bit it, drawing a gasp of surprise from her. Heal pooled through her to settle between her legs, a long-forgotten passion rising up in her.

His gaze caught hers, heavy-lidded and full of promise. Her breath halted and for a moment, she thought time stopped, too.

His lips crashed down on hers, with little of the sure and careful laziness he'd had the night before. Shocked by the suddenness of it, Ivy couldn't respond for half a second. It had been so long since she'd been held or kissed that for a horrible moment, she thought she'd forgotten what to do. Instinct took over, urging her to wrap her arms around him to pull him closer, the feel of his body through her thin nightgown an absolute thrill. She could hardly wait to know what it would feel like, skin to skin with him.

Merritt's tongue swept into her mouth with a fierce

possession that took her breath away, drawing a gasp of surprise from her. He pulled away, his own breath short, then leaned his forehead against hers. "Ivy." His voice was a breathless whisper, raspy and hoarse.

It took a few seconds to find her own, and when she did all she could respond with was, "Mm?"

His fingers curled around her hips. "I…"

Her heart sank, a feeling that was at war with the need rippling through her. "Mm?"

"I want you."

She laughed, the sound nervous and shaky. "I would hope so. I want you, too."

"I've never… I haven't been intimate with a client before." His hips pushed against hers, the motion involuntary.

Ivy gasped again. "I won't tell."

"This will complicate things." He sounded apologetic, wistful.

She wondered how often he gave in to his own desires. "Complicated doesn't mean bad. Sometimes, it only means change." She held her breath, waiting for his reply.

It came after a silence that felt like it stretched on forever. "Change doesn't have to be bad, either."

Tension released from her shoulders and she relaxed a little. Only some of the tension, the part that was worried about rejection. The rest of her was still primed for activity, muscles taut as electric wires. "So, want me," she whispered.

His response was an unintelligible growl. His lips found hers again and she leaned into him, wanting more. His hands scrabbled for her hips again, pulling her up against him until her bare feet were nearly off the floor. On instinct, she wrapped one of her legs around his, then immediately regretted it when both of them nearly fell over. Before she could apologize, Merritt hauled her up so she could wrap her legs around his waist.

She stared at him, their faces now level with one another, astonished at the swift motion. His eyes were glassy with desire and she knew hers had to be, too. She held on to him, waiting to see what he would do next. She was surprised when took a few awkward steps to the desk where not half an hour ago she had been drinking chocolate and contemplating spells. He set her down on the desktop, a wicked gleam in his eye. One hand lazily crept up her nightgown, pushing the fabric aside as his calloused fingertips lightly scraped her skin, sending electric sparks skittering across it. He paused behind her knee, raising it just enough so he could comfortably stand between her legs.

He raised her other leg, his eyes never leaving hers.

She was grateful to be on the desk for fear that her legs couldn't support her. Ivy's fingers drifted down his shirt, toying with the buttons. Experimentally, she flicked open a few to reveal his skin.

One of his hands drifted upward, making her fingers halt on his chest. "May I?" he murmured.

Ivy wanted to scream "Yes!" but held back. She nodded and tried to form a verbal response, but Merritt's hand was sliding along her skin. She forgot how to speak.

He hovered on the spot where her thigh met her hip, gently stroking her bare skin. He made an appreciative noise as she twitched, then sucked in a harsh gasp under his careful touch, so close to where she wanted his hand yet so far.

When she found her voice, all she could whisper was, "Please."

He didn't make her beg, which she appreciated. His deft fingers slipped down the inside of her thigh, skimming her skin until he reached the heat between her legs. She whimpered in response as he found her, wet and wanting, trembling under him. His face was a curious mask of lust and concentration as he watched her reactions. Her hips involuntarily bucked against his hand and she bit back a soft cry of frustration. Every muscle and tendon in her body was at alert, desperate for release…

He slid a finger inside her and she nearly came undone on the desktop.

Clearly satisfied with her reactions so far, Merritt had a smug smile on his face as he withdrew his hand, then fell to the floor on his knees. He hooked one leg over his shoulder, and with a lewd thrill Ivy realized what he wanted to do. She knew what he was going to ask as soon as he opened his mouth. Before he could speak, she said, "Yes."

A devilish grin that she'd never seen from him before spread across his face. He pushed up her nightgown, exposing her to him. Ivy's pulse beat faster under his gaze, the need for him to touch her again overwhelming.

She nearly lifted herself off the desk when his mouth touched her warm center, exploring her like he had all the time in the world. In a strange way, it reminded her of the lane the night before, when she'd felt like a meal to him and he intended to savor her.

Oh, he *did*.

He gently sucked at her tender flesh, his hand returning to where it was before. He paused just long enough to slide his finger inside her again, moving in a way that made her wish he had something else of his inside her. Her fingers bunched in his hair, urging him on as he fastened his lips over her again, teasing another whimper out of her. She was dimly aware of him hooking her other leg over his shoulder as her back arched, pleasure coursing through her as Merritt licked and stroked her until she was on the edge of climax. He slowed, causing a wave of confusion and frustration to cascade through her. "Merritt?" Her voice was wobbly and sounded far away to her ears. She was very aware of the feel of his hair in her hands, his skin against hers, the feel of her nightgown pushed up around her waist.

His response was wordless, diving back in with a renewed enthusiasm. He murmured something unintelligible against her skin, sending tiny vibrations through her that she wouldn't have imagined could have such an impact. Her legs shook on either side of his head and he gripped them, holding her in place as he continued. She exploded against him, her orgasm crashing through her like a storm on a beach. Merritt didn't stop until she leaned back against the wall, wrung out.

It felt like hours had passed before she could right herself. As it was, she was able to hoist herself up on shaking arms as Merritt rose from the floor, a satisfied look on his face that she wanted to kiss off. When she found her voice, all she could say was, "Are you certain you aren't part incubus?"

He actually flushed at that comment.

His hair was awry from her fierce grip on it, his clothes askew. There was still a noticeable bulge at the front of his trousers that had to be painful. When she was sure her legs would support her, Ivy slid off the desk. Deliberately meeting Merritt's gaze, she slipped off her nightgown so she was fully naked. He made a strangled sound in his throat as he took her in, and didn't move when she slid her hand down his chest, past his trousers waistband to stroke his erection through the fabric. Her fingers reached for the buttons, unfastening them as deftly as she could before pulling the fabric apart. Her hand skimmed against his bare skin above his waistband, causing him to suck in a harsh breath when she reached for his drawers. To her surprise and disappointment, his hand clamped over hers, halting her in place. "Don't," he said. "If you keep this up, it'll be over before it starts."

"I thought it already did."

"Before it continues, then. Do you want to continue this on the desk or the bed?"

His voice was rough, full of promise, and Ivy knew that no matter what she picked it would be good. "The bed."

"Good choice, although I do enjoy a good fuck on a table occasionally." He started unfastening the rest of his shirt buttons matter-of-factly.

"I could go for the desk, in that case."

"Next time," he promised. His shirt unbuttoned, he swatted her arse, drawing a squeal from her. "Get on the bed."

Ivy was powerless to disobey. A fresh rush of renewed lust swelled inside her, sending anticipation tingling down her spine, as she stretched out on the bed, propping her head up in her hand. She watched Merritt undress, tossing aside his clothes and not caring where they landed. Finally, he joined her on the bed, crawling over her and caging her in. His hands pinned her wrists on either side of her head as he lowered his face to hers, kissing her with the same slow tenderness he'd shown the night before. His cock brushed her thigh, hot and hard against her. She reached for it, wrapping her hand around him. He moaned, lips crashing against hers as he thrust into her hand.

He surprised her again when he released her wrists and rolled away from her. He grabbed his cock with one hand and pumped it once, eyes fastened to hers. "Get on," he ordered.

A fresh thrill coursed through her at the notion. She straddled him, balancing herself on either side of his hips before lowering herself over his body. She reached for his cock, lining it up at her entrance, before she gently, cautiously started to take him inside her. She took her time, dragging it out as she adjusted to him, before sliding down with him seated fully inside her.

His face was a mask of concentration, hands gripping her hips as he fought for control.

Ivy raised herself up a few inches, then dropped back down on his body, causing both of them to cry out at the contact.

"Fuck me," he muttered. He let go of her hips, stretching out to press his hands against the bed's headboard. His eyes rolled back in his head for a second.

"I'd planned on doing just that." She rocked her hips again, drawing another moan and a hard thrust in response from him. "Oh, *God*."

Merritt took a couple of deep breaths, gathering himself. She understood because she had to do the same. He shifted his hips, then thrust upward, making her gasp again. "I think I've wanted this since the first time I saw you," he ground out as he repeated the motion.

All Ivy could do was moan in response.

"You feel amazing." Before she could reply in kind, he reached for her, pulling her face down to meet his. His kiss was fierce, possessive.

Ivy couldn't form the words to tell him he did, too, as the rational part of her brain shut down, instinct taking over. She and Merritt found a slow, steady rhythm as he slid in and out of her. Neither of them spoke as they explored each other's bodies. It was as if the rest of the world had ceased to exist, that nothing else mattered outside the walls of her room.

Familiar, welcome tension built in her again, another orgasm imminent. As if he could sense it, Merritt increased his pace, then dropped his hand between their bodies where they joined, exactly where she wanted the extra pressure. She cried out, needing more. He gave it until she came again, hard and breathless, gripping him tightly. Through her hazy vision she saw another self-satisfied smirk cross his face, an expression she was only too happy to kiss away.

"Loved that," he murmured against her lips.

Her heart fluttered in a way that had nothing to do with orgasms. Once again, she was at a loss for words as his thrusts increased again, his muscles bunching beneath her. He kissed her as he came, catching her lower lip in his teeth for a thrilling few seconds before he moaned her name against her mouth.

Ivy didn't dare move, never wanting to disentangle herself from him again. She wasn't sure how much time passed before their breathing slowed back to normal. Gently, she pulled away from him to lie on her side. He wordlessly pulled her back to him to lay her head on his chest. His heartbeat was strong and steady under her ear. Outside, a light autumn rain started to beat against the windows.

Finally, Merritt said, "I didn't come here expecting that."

She couldn't keep the smile out of her voice. "I'm glad we did."

"So am I." He reached for the bedsheet and tucked it around them. "Next time, on the desk."

# CHAPTER 12

Ivy GAVE Merritt a knowing smile in the lift, and it was all he could do not to kiss it off her face. Even in her widow's weeds, she looked resplendent.

He couldn't believe he'd whiled away the afternoon in her hotel room with her, nor could he recall the last time he'd spent that much time in such a pleasurable way. It was only as the sky grew darker outside that they bathed and dressed for supper. Ben and Elora Lang were meeting them at the hotel's restaurant.

The other couple was already waiting for them at the restaurant in a private dining room. Both of them wore clothing that Merritt, the last person on the planet with any sense of fashion, could tell was not made in England. Elora's deep blue gown matched the color of her eyes. It contrasted nicely with her blond hair, worn loose and curled around her face. A matching blue ribbon was wound around her throat, undoubtedly to hide the puncture marks left by her vampire husband. Ben's suit was a dark charcoal, perfectly cut, his white shirt snowy and pristine. Other than appearing a little pale, nothing gave him away as a vampire.

Ben stood up when Merritt and Ivy approached, offering a bow to her that felt a little ostentatious. The vampire was nothing if not a little dramatic, Merritt thought wryly. His hackles rose when Ben kissed Ivy's hand, an irrational feeling of jealousy. He was ever the incorrigible flirt, even in undeath.

If Elora noticed, she didn't care. Instead, she raised a knowing eyebrow in Merritt's direction as he helped Ivy into her seat.

He wondered what he'd given away. He quickly answered his own question as he thought about his reflection in her room's looking glass as they'd readied themselves for dinner. He couldn't remember the last time he'd looked upon himself to see the worry lines around his eyes smoothed away, nor a smile on his face. Certainly not before this afternoon.

"Thank you for coming tonight," Elora said once they were all seated around the table. She gave Ben's hand an affectionate squeeze next to her. To Ivy, she said, "Merritt says you're in a bit of a bind."

A muscle in Ivy's jaw ticked. "That's the polite way to describe it."

"I already asked Merritt this, but is there anything we can do to help?"

Any answer Ivy might have had was silenced when a waiter let himself into the dining room to take orders. "Red wine for me," Ben said. In a low voice Merritt could only think of as hypnotic, he added, "You will not think my not eating is unusual."

Elora rolled her eyes and ordered beef.

When the waiter left and no one else was in earshot,

Elora sighed. "This is a nice restaurant. No one would have cared much that you aren't eating."

"I'm working on my glamoring skills." Changing the subject, Ben said, "You didn't answer. Is there anything we can do to help?"

Merritt and Ivy exchanged a glance. "Doubtful, but thank you for offering," Merritt replied.

"What's happened so far?" Elora nudged him a little with her elbow, and Ben looked at Ivy as if remembering his manners. "My apologies, I know you're still in mourning."

"Half-mourning," Ivy murmured, with an unreadable glance at Merritt. Whether it was because she obviously wasn't wearing head to toe black or he'd spent the afternoon enthusiastically making love to her, he couldn't tell. Her voice stronger, she added, "We have to figure out a way to release my late husband's soul from wherever trapped, find out how he really died, and ensure that his patent medicine formulation stays the way he intended." She said the words matter-of-factly, as if reciting them from a list.

Damn it all, Merritt had forgotten all about the Miracle Elixir in his quest to stop Penright. He'd forgotten about Edwin Thaddeus, the man himself, too, having reduced him to a trapped spirit while he lusted after his wife. Guilt twanged through him, and with it, doubt and regret. It wasn't enough that he had actually slept with a client—a first for him—but he'd slept with the widow of a man possibly murdered for financial gain, whose soul he hoped to free.

Gods above and below, would that ever be an awkward conversation when he finally met Dr. Thaddeus.

Ivy changed the subject, turning to Ben. "Is it terribly impolite to ask how you're finding life as a vampire?"

The vampire's response was swift. "Not at all. Would it be impolite to ask what you are? Sloan has only recently acknowledged that he could raise me from daylight sleep."

"I've never actually done that," Merritt quickly said. "I'm still not certain I could." Although it would have been a useful skill to have when he was tracking vampires across England, investigating the bloodshed in their wake, when he met Ben and Elora.

"I'm a witch," Ivy replied.

"Huh." Ben leaned forward, clearly intrigued. "What kind of spells can you cast?"

"I'm a healer."

"Could you make, I don't know, the flames larger?" Ben gestured to the pair of candlesticks in the middle of the table. Real candles, not the flameless ones from Scotland that were currently all the rage.

"I don't see why not." Before any of them could react, Ivy recited a few words in a language Merritt didn't recognize. The flames glowed, then exploded into a riot of heat and colors for a heart-stopping second. As quickly as the show began, the flames were reduced to their original size.

Elora touched her eyebrows, then her nose. "Has my face melted off?"

Merritt couldn't help but do the same, relief pouring through him when his fingers touched unsinged eyelashes and intact skin. He glanced at Ivy, who had a satisfied grin on her face, one he wanted to kiss off her. Still, he couldn't help but ask, "What the hell was that?"

She smiled, the expression far more serene than he would have expected. "Witch magic."

The waiter returned with their food, heedless to the near-inferno in the private dining room. Conversation ceased as they ate, save for Ben's disappointed sigh as he looked on enviously at their dinners. "Do you actually get hungry?" Ivy asked.

If he'd been capable of it, Ben might have blushed. "Not in the way I did when I was still alive." He and Elora exchanged a knowing look. Ivy didn't push for more details.

"The Walker Art Gallery is hosting a late night exhibition this evening," Ben said. "It's so rare to see English galleries thinking of the hours their undead patrons keep. We're going to take a cab there after supper. Would you like to join us?"

"A *steam* cab. Not an ornithopter." Elora emphasized, reminding Merritt of how she'd discovered her fear of heights shortly after they met.

He glanced at Ivy, unsure how to answer. Part of him wanted to take her back to her room and not leave for another day or two. Another, more practical part reminded him that they still had work to do to free Dr. Thaddeus. Work she had been poring over, when he thought of the spells in her room, that he'd so rudely interrupted. Try as he might, he couldn't bring himself to regret that.

Ivy must have been thinking along the same lines. "We're so close to a breakthrough with this case," she said apologetically.

Merritt let out a breath he hadn't realized he was holding. He liked Ben and Elora, considered them friends and he didn't have a lot of them. Perhaps on another night, when he wasn't preoccupied with this and Ivy wasn't still in half-mourning, when he could take her out for a proper evening like a gentleman, they could take a trip to a gallery. He'd never considered a future with a woman before. The very notion of one was a little terrifying, but comforting, in an odd way. His necromancy skills and knack for attracting ghosts kept him avoiding all but the most superficial of relationships until he met Ivy.

She and Elora excused themselves to go to the ladies' room after their plates were cleared, leaving him and Ben alone in the dining room. "She's very nice," Ben said when they were out of earshot.

"I think so, too."

"You seem happy." The vampire leaned back in his chair as he said the words, a smile on his face, as if he'd just solved an impossible riddle.

Merritt shrugged, hoping he hid his nervousness over his complicated feelings with Ivy. "She's certainly the most informed client I've ever had. It's nice not having to lie about why I can determine the true cause of someone's death so quickly."

Ben lifted a dark eyebrow in response, his expression unreadable. Merritt wondered what Elora had told him before dinner. Probably everything and then some, given that they were married and blood-bonded for eternity. Couples that close wouldn't keep things from each other.

Could he and Ivy ever share that closeness? Usually a private man, Merritt didn't find that idea unappealing.

Ivy and Elora returned, wide-eyed and ashen-faced to Merritt's consternation. Alarm threaded through him. "What is it?" he asked, immediately leaping to his feet.

Ivy sighed. "You'll never guess who's here in the public dining room."

Merritt's heart sank. There was only one person who could put that look on her face. "God fucking damn it."

"What's going on?" Ben asked.

"Dr. Thaddeus's business partner is here," Elora explained.

"How the hell did he know we were here?" Merritt asked.

"This isn't exactly an obscure hotel or restaurant," Elora replied.

She was right, but that knowledge didn't rankle him any less.

"It's worse than that," Ivy said. Merritt braced himself, knowing what was next. "He's dining with Penright and Ezra."

Merritt hadn't been expecting to hear Ezra Thaddeus's name and it took a couple of seconds for it to sink in. "Fucking hell."

"Who's Ezra again?" Ben asked.

"My stepson. The one who's been accusing me of murder." Ivy sighed again. She looked and sounded like she was on the verge of tears. "None of them spotted us when we were walking to and from the retiring room. Ezra would have made a scene if he saw me. But we have to leave as soon as possible, and it's not because of me." She gave a pointed look to Ben.

"You don't think he would do something to me in public and what both of us are?" Ben asked, but there was a note of uncertainty in his voice.

Ivy's reply was steady, her voice simmering with anger. "He's placed my husband's soul into some kind of purgatory and killed my housekeeper. He may have killed other people. He summons souls from the afterlife for fun. Yes, I think he's capable of doing something terrible in public and getting away with it." To Merritt, she asked, "What could a necromancer do to a vampire?"

He was unsure how to answer, not having ever summoned a vampire before. "Theoretically, raise him during daylight hours." Elora cried out a little and grabbed Ben's arm, even though she had to already know that. "I'm not certain otherwise, since our skills lie with spirits and not physical bodies. The magic to that has to exist, though."

"Which is why we need to get out of here now. We've wasted enough time already," said Elora. She reached for her coat hanging from the tree in the corner of the room, but Ben was faster. He helped her into it. "I've already settled our accounts."

For some stupid reason, that statement pricked Merritt's masculine pride. "I'm sorry?"

"I took care of dinner as soon as Ivy pointed out the necromancer. I invited you out tonight, anyway," Elora said in a tone that brooked no argument. "Ben and I are going to leave through the restaurant's back door through the kitchen. We don't know if this other necromancer can sense vampires the same way Merritt can."

"There's bound to be garlic in the kitchens," Ben muttered.

"All garlic will do is make your eyes water. You can glamor anyone who questions our being in there. We'll be fast, anyway." To Ivy and Merritt, Elora said, "Will you be all right to go back to the hotel?"

"You're still going to the gallery?"

Ben and Elora exchanged a glance. "I doubt necromancers will skulk about an exhibit of modern erotic art," Ben replied.

Merritt was forced to admit he was probably correct. He was also uncertain about how much protection the vampire and his wife could provide, outside of his enhanced strength. "We'll be fine to return to the hotel on our own."

"Very well. Come with us, then." Once again, Elora's tone was commanding.

The four of them slipped out of the dining room, following Elora through the restaurant to the kitchen. Ben occasionally locked eyes with surprised waiters, telling them that they had no memory of them as they rushed through. The vampire gagged in the kitchen at the potent scent of garlic, interrupting him as he commanded the cooks to forget that they were ever there, and took deep, dramatic breaths as they burst through the restaurant's back door into the night air. Any freshness in it was marred by the stink of the alley they'd found themselves in. The scents of rotting food and rodents were nearly over-powering.

They hurried out of the alley to the street, where there was no trace of the group they'd just escaped from. A couple of steam cabs idled at the curb, and Merritt flagged one with a wave of his hand. "That's us," he said, waiting next to it.

"It was good to see you," Ben replied, holding out his hand for Merritt to shake. "Ivy, it was nice to meet you."

Merritt clasped Ben's hand in response. Even though he knew what the other man was, the coolness of his skin surprised him. He had the body temperature of a marble statue.

He gave Elora a hug goodbye before he and Ivy slipped into the waiting cab. Neither of them spoke during the short journey back to the hotel, and Merritt collected his thoughts as the vehicle lumbered along the streets. Part of him wished he'd been able to catch a glimpse of the trio, see what their body language said, perhaps even catch some of their conversation if he could get close enough. Would they speak openly of money and spirits in such a public place? Did Ezra even believe in spirits?

A pair of ghosts, both men in old-fashioned evening clothes, floated past them as they walked through the hotel's lobby, the first time Merritt had seen any in hotel. They blinked in surprise at the sight of Merritt, and one nodded in his direction before they resumed their murmured conversation. "Far too loud," Merritt heard as they passed them. "The state of the youth today…"

He bit back a smile. Some complaints were evergreen.

Any mirth quickly evaporated when they reached Ivy's door. She hesitated in front of it, her brass room key hovering over the lock. "Is something wrong?" Merritt asked.

"Yes, but I'm not sure what." She looked on either side of her, up and down the corridor. "Are there any ghosts here?"

He couldn't sense anything untoward, but his scope of power was limited. "Aside from the gents in fifty-year-old evening wear in the lobby, no. They didn't follow us. What's wrong?"

Worry lines bracketed her mouth. "Someone's been in my room. My protection spell has been breached."

"Fuck." Merritt stared at the door, wishing he could be more helpful. "Is anyone in there now?"

Ivy uttered a short spell, her Latin fluent. Despite the gravity of the situation, Merritt couldn't help but be impressed, as he always was when she rattled something off in another language. "There's no one inside, nor have any other spells been set," she reported. The lines of worry didn't smooth from her features. "At least, nothing I could sense."

"Is it safe for me to go in?" Merritt asked.

"It's my room."

"And it's my case."

She placed the key in the lock. "Edwin was my husband."

Merritt put his hand over hers, delaying her unlocking the door. "Let me check the room first," he said. "Believe it or not, I'm qualified to do this."

She narrowed her eyes at him and shook her head a

little. "If it will assuage your ego, I'll let you go in first but I'll be right behind you."

That was good enough for Merritt. Ivy stepped aside and let him unlock the door.

The room appeared as it was when they left: the bed unmade, Ivy's nightgown crumpled at the foot of it. The dishes she'd been eating from before he arrived were exactly where she left them. Heat rose in him when he remembered how they'd finished her plate of biscuits between bouts of lovemaking earlier in the day. He quickly forced the memory out of his mind, albeit reluctantly. Being with Ivy had truly ruined his ability to focus.

"Someone was here," Ivy repeated, snapping him back to the present. "I can't tell who it was, but it was likely Penright." She picked up the folder of spells she'd left on the desk and leafed through it. "Ha! He didn't touch them." Her voice had a note of satisfaction to it that Merritt wouldn't have expected at such a time.

"How do you know what he was looking for?"

"What else could it have been? Nothing's been taken. Perhaps he was looking for a proper grimoire, not a leather folder of unseelie fae spells written on foolscap."

"Perhaps he didn't know what they were or he copied them."

"Or he wasn't looking for them at all." Her voice had a faraway quality, like she was speaking to herself rather than him. "What if he had come here to kill me like he originally intended to at my house?"

It was a horrific notion, but plausible. "You're no longer safe here," Merritt said.

It took a few seconds for his words to sink in. She squeezed her eyes shut in frustration, collecting herself. "Where the hell else would I be safe?" She sounded like she was near tears.

"My flat, at least until we find a new hiding spot for you."

"And then what? I move again, and again, until he finally kills me and McCann can take over the company? Ezra gets his wish for a dead stepmother? No." Ivy shook her head. "I'll leave with you tonight, but we have to find another solution to this and I don't think it'll be within human law."

"We have the spells to consider. There must be a way to combine our magic."

"I'm certain there is, but I don't think I have enough time." Ivy started gathering her things to pack. "We'll have to kill Penright."

# CHAPTER 13

THE QUESTION of how things had gone so spectacularly wrong wouldn't stop tumbling through Ivy's head throughout the journey back to Merritt's flat. She had spent a luxurious day in bed with him, then met his friends, only for everything to deteriorate so quickly. It had been a holiday from reality, nothing more. Her anger at her hotel room being breached welled up again when Merritt escorted her into his flat, locking the door behind them. "Do you suppose we're safe here?" she couldn't help but ask as he lit one of his electric lamps.

"I think so. Claudia, has anyone visited the building or my flat?"

Ah, yes. Ivy had forgotten about Merritt's flatmate.

"Claudia says that no one has been by today and she'll keep an eye out for unwelcome visitors."

"Thank you, Claudia." Ivy felt a bit silly speaking to the open air, but wanted to be polite. A slight breeze drifted across her face, a faint trace of frankincense in the air for a few seconds in response. Ivy couldn't help but shiver.

"She says you're welcome." Merritt's expression shifted and she wondered what the ghost was telling him.

He picked up Ivy's bag and carried it to his bedroom. The sight was reassuring. "Not exactly," he said, then another pause. "No, we're fine for now, but Mrs. Thaddeus's situation is becoming more dire. Her housekeeper has already been killed and we think the man who did it is after her next." He returned to the sitting room and asked Ivy, "Could I get you a drink?"

Ivy nodded. "Thank you."

In the kitchen, Merritt poured short drinks for each of them while continuing his conversation with Claudia. "Of course, we can't stay here too long. It's just for the night." He recapped the whiskey bottle. "We're still sorting out what to do next." He gave Ivy a warm look, one that said he would protect her as best he could. Her heart fluttered at the sight, hopeful thing it was. "We have spells to work through. Which reminds me, I don't know what they can do to ghosts who've stayed on the mortal plane by choice." He returned to the sitting room and handed Ivy her glass. "It might be for the best tonight. Even if a necromancer wasn't running about killing people and trapping spirits, I'd be asking you to do that."

Ivy was dying to know what Claudia was saying, but she didn't ask. She took a sip of her drink and enjoyed the burn it left in her throat.

"No one's going to force you to do anything before you're ready." Another pause. "I appreciate that. I'll call for you if I need you." He sat down heavily on the sofa. Ivy joined him. He leaned back and closed his eyes. "She's gone."

"Not permanently, I hope."

"No, just across the corridor to the empty flat for now. I also didn't mean to put the fear of God in her about

Penright or our unseelie spells. She's terrified of being trapped or forced into the afterlife."

That introduced an entirely new fear into Ivy. "I hope we don't accidentally do that."

"We won't."

Ivy wished she had the confidence Merritt did. She retrieved the folder of spells from her luggage and passed a few of the foolscap sheets to him. She could sense the power the incantations held, but didn't dare repeat the words for fear of unleashing hell. "Some of the spells are in Vulgar Latin dialects I can't understand, nor can I place where it originates."

"That could be an unseelie dialect." He sat next to her and picked up one of the spells. Even through her layers of skirts, she could feel his body heat, a distraction she couldn't afford right now.

"That seems likely, but I don't want to try casting a spell whose words I can't understand."

"Do you recognize anything at all?" He hesitated, and Ivy waited for him to continue before answering. "I sort of didn't get around to discussing this with you earlier today like I intended."

Her heart flip-flopped at the thought of how they spent the afternoon. She leafed through the pages. "I found a couple of spells with words similar to the Latin dialect I use. They looked like domestic incantations. Spells for heating water, alchemy, healing, but I can't be certain."

"Alchemy?"

"That's what I think it says. *Elchymae* is close enough to *alchimiae.* The rest of the spell references words that look like the Latin terms for tin and copper." A thought seized her. "Perhaps Claudia could help."

"She's scared to death…" He quickly caught himself. "Well, not quite."

"Does she still speak Latin?"

Understanding dawned on Merritt. "I feel like an idiot."

"So do I."

"I can't believe I didn't think to ask for her help with translating." He rose. "Excuse me."

He crossed the room to the flat's door and opened it. "Claudia?" His voice was a stage whisper. "No, everything's fine." A moment later he stepped back into the sitting room and closed the door. "She's here," he said to Ivy.

Unsure of the manners surrounding specters, Ivy said, "Hello, Claudia."

"Claudia says hello to you, too." Merritt collected the foolscap and spread the sheets out on the table in front of the sofa. "You asked earlier if there was anything you could help us with. We didn't think to ask if you remembered Latin." There was a pause, then a faint chill slipped past Ivy that lasted only a second or two. "Ivy speaks some of it for her spells, but she doesn't recognize these dialects."

There was another, lengthier pause. Merritt adjusted some of the pages without comment. "Truly?" He looked up in wonder.

Ivy was dying to ask him what caught his attention, but refrained from it. She leaned forward to better see the ancient papers.

"No, that's more than what we have to go on. This is incredible." He brushed away a few of the pages, making a neat stack and pushing it to the side. "You don't have to apologize for anything. We have a lot to work with." He straightened and gave a grateful smile to the air. "Thank you so much. I promise I won't get either of us killed, too." To Ivy, he said, "Claudia says a lot of these are rubbish spells for trickery and deception, which makes sense since they're from the unseelie fae. These ones are for necromancy." He collected the loose pages from the tabletop and slid them across to Ivy.

Of course, the necromancy spells would be on the pages that she hated to hold most of all. She could *feel* their darkness, the misery they could inflict. She wanted to toss them away. "What do they do?"

"This one summons spirits from the afterlife. Not the way I do," he quickly clarified. "I ask permission first. This one just sort of… yanks them out of the ether, I suppose, then shoves them back where they came from with hardly so much a by-your-leave."

"Claudia could pick all of that up in this bastardized Latin?"

Merritt's eyes flicked from Ivy's to the space where she guessed the ghost stood. "She says there's enough similarity between the Latin she spoke when she was alive to the fae version here for her to understand enough of it. She also says that just because she's dead and forced to speak English with me doesn't mean her literacy skills in her first language have also died."

"My apologies, Claudia."

"She also wants me to tell you that English is the worst excuse of a language she's ever heard."

"Understood. I reiterate my apologies."

"She says she accepts your apology, and wants us to take note that *this* spell—" He held up a sheet, so old that the ink used to write the words had nearly faded— "Can be used to resurrect a ghost into human form."

If Ivy hadn't already been sitting, her knees would have given way. "What?"

"It requires some hard to find ingredients and raw innate power that doesn't exist anymore, but this spell can bring a ghost into physical form and retain it indefinitely."

He regarded the foolscap thoughtfully. "Although I suppose when I think about it, it isn't that far removed from raising the dead."

"Have you ever done that?" His expression darkened and she immediately regretted asking. "Never mind. What about the others?"

"This other spell traps souls and holds them in a place of the necromancer's choosing."

Ivy forgot about Merritt's misadventures in raising the dead. She straightened. "Like how Penright trapped Edwin's soul."

"It could be, although this particular spell refers to physically trapping souls. Keeping them in physical vessels rather than between planes. Claudia says there's nothing here that could do that."

"Could the trapping spell be reversed? Every witch's grimoire I've ever consulted has a reversal spell, as well."

Merritt held out the paper to where Claudia had to be and waited for an answer. "Yes, there are a couple of methods of reversal, one of which is a spell and the other simply breaking the vessels. No other rituals needed."

It almost sounded too easy. "All we have to do to release Edwin is break whatever he's been kept in?"

"Not necessarily. We don't know which spells are holding them and if they need to be reversed with more magic. We also don't know for certain that he isn't simply trapped between planes. Claudia says there's nothing here that can help with that." He sighed. "Or we can simply kill Penright and find out if doing so undoes everything he's caused. You even suggested it earlier tonight."

She had. While Ivy wanted to see Edwin freed and his patent medicine legacy live on, the thought of taking a life still felt horrific. She wasn't sure she had it in her to do that. "I did." She hated the wobble in her voice.

Merritt set down the foolscap and sat next to her, taking her hands in his. "Ivy."

She focused on his warmth, the *life* she could feel beneath his skin. She focused on his hands, his slim, sure fingers. They'd done incredible things to her body earlier in the day. Perhaps it was a mistake to focus on them. "Yes?"

"I don't think we're getting out of this without spilling blood. Remember, we're doing this because someone stole your husband's afterlife, his business, and tried to kill you." Despite the gravity of his words, his voice was reassuring, if apologetic.

"Have you ever killed anyone?"

"Yes, I've killed vampires." There was a telltale pause, and she wondered what Claudia was saying. "That's quite all right. You've been very helpful. Thank you again." A few seconds later, he said, "She's left for the night."

"What did she say?"

"She asked if I needed any more help, because we obviously have some things to discuss. To answer your earlier question, yes, I raised someone from the dead. That's how I found out I'm a necromancer." Pain and regret lanced his voice. "My grandfather lived with us when I was a boy. He passed in the night of old age in his bed, nothing nefarious. I said my goodbyes to him and dearly wished that I could sit down and read with him one last time, and he woke from the dead."

A chill slithered down Ivy's spine. "My God."

"My parents were beside themselves. I was about five years old and necromancy powers don't usually manifest until later."

"What did your grandfather say?"

"He told me to put him back to sleep and never to do that again. I was crying, of course, and it took a few moments for me to understand that I had to wish my grandfather dead again to put him back to sleep. Shortly after that, my parents started teaching me correct necromancy techniques."

"How horrible for you. I can't imagine." Ivy was suddenly very grateful that her skills were easily controlled.

"I'd been seeing ghosts before that happened, although one of my parents was always with me when I was little and they'd get bothersome spirits to leave me be." That shadowed look was back on his face, and her heart ached at the thought of what he'd gone through as a child. "Desperate ghosts don't care if the person who can see them is a child."

"I'm sorry."

"Don't be. It was a long time ago and I have a handle on things now."

"And we'll handle this by killing Penright." She felt sick again after saying the words.

"Ivy, I will do everything in my power not to have to do that. I don't relish the idea of killing someone." He stroked the back of hand with the pad of his thumb. The motion was tiny, but it sent sparks skittering across her flesh, distracting her once again. "We have some very old unseelie magic at our disposal, and with it, I think we're evenly matched with Penright."

"How do we find him? How does this end?"

"I'll find out where he lives and we'll work from there. That's in my wheelhouse."

Merritt made it sound so easy. She desperately wanted to believe that this could be resolved as simply as he was proposing. Find Penright's home and take him by surprise.

"What if he comes here?" she couldn't help but ask.

"We'll go to another place to hide. A hotel, rent a room in a boarding house, we'll have options. I promise being on the run won't last too long." As if to emphasize his point, he kissed her for the first time since before dinner.

Ivy's response was immediate. Her arms looped around his neck, pulling him closer to her, tongue tangling with his, needing to feel close to him again. Her first impulse was to pull at his clothes, let him take her here on his sofa, but practicality took over. She reluctantly broke the kiss before they could get carried away, then threaded her fingers through his. "Thank you," she murmured.

"No thanks necessary. I care about you as a friend."

She couldn't keep away a bubble of laughter from welling up inside her. "Are we friends?" God, but it felt good to laugh, even if it was only for a moment.

"I'm unsure what we are, but friends, confidantes—yes. We can have more than one word to describe what we are." He rose and she did the same, not letting go of him. She needed the support, the connection. "Tomorrow morning, we'll find out more about Penright and how he operates. We'll take him by surprise."

Speaking of surprise… he was leading her to his bedroom. "Am I sleeping here tonight?"

"Of course, unless you'd prefer the sofa. It might be too short for you, though."

Merritt switched on an oil lamp, bathing his bedroom in warm yellow light. It was tidy and spare, like the rest of the flat, the bed neatly made up. "Stay with me," he said.

She felt herself flush, and a warm feeling spread through her that had nothing to do with what they could be doing in the bed for the rest of the night. His words sounded almost like a plea, like he needed her. "Yes."

# CHAPTER 14

T HE MORNING DAWNED gray and dreary. A light rain misted outside, and the knowledge that someone was out to kill the woman still sleeping next to him was never far from Merritt's mind. However, the danger, the miserable weather, the work still ahead of them… all of that weight was lifted, if only for a moment, as he took in the sight of the woman whose head rested on the pillow next to his. Merritt couldn't remember the last time he'd spent the night with someone. He tucked a strand of hair behind her ear. Taking pains not to disturb her, climbed out of bed and slipped on his robe.

He shut the bedroom door behind him and started making tea. While the water was set to boil on the steam-powered stove, the familiar scent of frankincense-laced perfume filled the air. He didn't bother to turn around. "Good morning, Claudia."

"I'm still here, so I presume neither you nor your lady friend cast any dark fae banishing spells last night."

"Of course not. Thank you again for your help, by the way."

Claudia materialized next to the stove. "You've let me pester you for as long as I've stayed here, so it was the least I could do."

"You haven't pestered me. You've always been the most polite ghost I've ever known." He measured tea leaves into a pot instead of just dumping them into a cup like he usually did.

"I wanted to let you know that someone stood outside the building for a while last night." Claudia's voice wavered, and with it, Merritt's heart squeezed. He hated seeing his friend afraid. Just as he hated being stalked.

"God damn it," he muttered.

"He didn't come in and I didn't get a very good look at him. I didn't want him to know I was there. I went downstairs into Mrs. Malton's flat and watched him from her sitting room window."

"You didn't disturb Mrs. Malton?" The elderly widowed landlady had claimed that the building was haunted since before Merritt moved in. Of course, it *was* haunted, although the ghost who did so wasn't malicious. The landlady probably had some fae blood in her from a few generations back, if she could sense Claudia's presence.

Claudia looked affronted at the suggestion. "Of course not. I'd rather not startle anyone into the grave if I can help it. Then I would have to share haunting duties with someone else." She shook her head. "I'm getting distracted. A man stood in front of the building last night, about half past one, for perhaps ten minutes. I think he cast a spell, but I couldn't hear him to be sure."

Merritt's blood ran cold. "Why do you think that?"

"His hand motions." Claudia mimicked what she'd seen, transparent hands waving in the air. To Merritt's unpracticed eye, the gestures did look like spellcasting.

"Did you get a good look at him?"

"No. I could only see his form under the streetlamp. I saw a tall man, wearing a long dark overcoat and bowler hat, like yours. He had that halo about his head like you do."

Merritt closed his eyes, breathed deeply in an attempt to center himself. "A necromancer."

"I think he was, but I was too far away to be sure."

No one but necromancers would have that tell for ghosts. "Damn it. I hoped we had a day or two before we had to worry about Penright showing up here." In retrospect, it was a stupid notion. The man moved faster than Merritt expected. He thought about poor Martha's murder and felt like an idiot. The water boiled. He poured it into the pot over the tea leaves. He let himself be momentarily distracted by the warm, pleasant scent. "We'll have to leave again," he mused aloud as he arranged the teapot and a pair of cups on a tray. "Thank you for looking out for us."

"You're welcome." An uncharacteristic shy look crossed her features. "Thank you for being my friend."

Merritt was oddly touched at her words. "You're welcome? Thank you for being mine, as well. This line of work doesn't allow much in the way of friendships."

"You could have ignored me or exorcised me if you really wanted to. Or moved to another flat. Instead, you've invited me in and treated me like a person. I appreciate that."

"I don't exorcise people." Not for the first time, Merritt wondered what she'd experienced in her life during the time of the Roman Empire, what made her stay on the mortal plane as long as she had. He didn't pry—he never did—but he still hoped that one day she would tell him. If she still remembered, that was. Sometimes, a ghost wandered the mortal plane so long that they forgot why.

"I know, and I wanted you to know that I appreciate that." She placed a ghostly hand on Merritt's arm, a friendly gesture that made him shiver involuntarily. "Be safe out there. This is the first time you've ever had to go head to head with another necromancer."

Didn't Merritt know that. He'd faced supernatural creatures before, mostly vampires, and investigated that abandoned laboratory where shifters were experimented upon, but never one of his own. "I will be," he promised.

"Good."

Any rejoinder Merritt might have offered was forgotten when Ivy padded into the kitchen. Despite the danger she was in, he couldn't help the desire that threaded through him at the sight of her. What would it be like, waking up next to her every morning? "I smelled tea," she said, yawning.

He hated what he was going to have to tell her. "I have tea and bad news." He may as well get it over with.

Any trace of sleepiness immediately evaporated. "Don't tell me Penright has already found us."

"He has, and we'll leave the flat this morning. Claudia saw him last night."

Her face fell, and for a moment he thought she might cry. "God damn it."

"Come here." Merritt held out his arms and she leaned into him, wrapping hers around his neck. She fit perfectly against him, the feel of her and the fragrance of her hair other distractions he couldn't afford right now. He needed the contact and knew she did, too. "We'll get to the bottom of this, I promise."

She sank into him for a moment like he was a lifeline, a discouraged sigh escaping her. She raised her head. "I was thinking about paying Ezra a visit today."

"Whatever for?"

Ivy gave him a look that clearly questioned his intelligence. "To find out why he hired Penright."

"That isn't safe."

"Ezra's a lot of things, but I know he wouldn't physically hurt me. Both of us know that he didn't try to orchestrate my murder. He's grieving and irrational. He's never believed in the paranormal before, so I don't understand why he would get involved with a necromancer."

"Penright and Ezra were both with McCann last night," Merritt pointed out. "It's reasonable to assume that McCann influenced Ezra."

"I'm going to speak to him today," Ivy replied. "He'll be at his flat this time of day." She pulled away from him and poured herself a cup of tea.

"I'd planned on making a visit to Penright's paranormal museum. We can go visit Ezra later."

She shook her head. "No, I go alone to visit Ezra."

Alarm flared through him. "Absolutely not."

"Yes." Her voice was firm, brooking no argument. "He won't speak to me if you're there."

"He hardly speaks to you at all!"

She sighed. "I don't hate him, Merritt. If anything, I feel sorry for him. He's faced a tremendous loss with Edwin's death and hasn't been able to grieve for distrust of me." She took a tentative sip of tea. "I think I'm going to tell him what kind of relationship Edwin and I had. If he's involved with Penright, he needs to know what he did to his father."

"No." The word escaped Merritt before he could form a more dignified, reasoned response.

"Excuse me?" Ivy's voice had taken a different note, one he hadn't heard before.

Oh, he'd fucked up. "Why don't we go together, and I can wait outside his flat in case anything happens?"

"I'm an adult. I have means of protecting myself. Just because I use my gifts for healing doesn't mean I can't be a threat in my own right." Ivy set her cup down with a little more force than necessary. She stared at it in surprise for a few seconds.

"I'm worried for you. McCann and Penright have both proven to be dangerous." Why wouldn't he stop talking? He'd never been this protective over someone before.

"And I won't be dealing with McCann or Penright, will I?" She narrowed her eyes at him. "It's a morning visit. His valet or cook will likely be at his flat, anyway. You can go to the museum, dig around it as you like, and we'll meet later in the day to compare notes."

Her voice hadn't lost that angry edge. Merritt hoped he hadn't caused a permanent rift between them. "I'm sorry," he said, voice soft.

"I'm glad to hear it. You should be."

"I worry about you. I care about you more than you know." His feelings were quickly freefalling into something deeper than merely caring about her, but he didn't mention that.

Something in her expression softened. "I care about you, as well. I also care about your independence. I need you to respect mine, too."

He let out a relieved sigh. Some of the tension he'd been holding in his shoulders loosened. "I will. I do. I just don't like the idea of you visiting your stepson, telling him you're a witch, and hoping he'll take that news well."

Her eyes glazed over for a moment, as if lost in thought. "He deserves to know. He needs to know that I cared about his father. He was my best friend, I think. I don't have a lot of them." She shook her head, her eyes regaining their focus. "Excluding you, of course."

"Are we friends, then?" He couldn't keep a teasing note out of his voice.

"I think we both know we're more than that." She smiled. His heart squeezed, then sank with her next words. "And right now, we have to get ready to face our enemies."

CAUTION HAD Ivy occasionally checking over her shoulder as she strode through Liverpool's streets later that morning. A pale sun had risen, its weak light an odd beacon of hope, that this nightmare might finally start drawing to a close. Had it all been a nightmare, though? Even in bad dreams, good things could happen. Like Merritt, who fussed over her in a way no one else had, but still respected her abilities. He hadn't argued with her too much when she told him she would visit Ezra alone. She wasn't afraid of her stepson before and she wasn't now.

Ezra lived in a new flat in Allerton, a modern home that took up the first floor in a four-story building. He had a small garden in front, blooming with imported ornamental flowers that had been well taken care of by someone else. It was here that Ivy found him, sitting on an iron chair, a cheroot in one hand and a cup of tea in the other, a newspaper spread out in front of him on a matching iron table. He started when he saw her walk into the garden, lips downturned in disgust. "Why are you here?" he asked by way of greeting.

"May we talk in private?" Ivy kept her voice soft and level, hoping to placate him.

"What for?" He stubbed out his cheroot in a small brass tray half-filled with ashes.

"It's about your father."

"I assumed it would be. We have nothing in common but him."

"Ezra, this is very important and concerns both of our safety." She took a deep breath, steeling herself. "Your father and I were not entirely honest with you over the years, and it's time that I explained what happened between us. Could we speak in private in your home?"

He held up his hands and gestured around the immaculately kept garden. "Is this not private enough?"

"No. I'd like to sit down inside, away from any prying eyes or ears, and tell you everything. You deserve to know what you've gotten yourself into with Roger McCann and that Penright fellow."

Confusion crossed Ezra's features. "How the devil do you know about Penright?"

"That's why I have to speak to you in private. He's a very dangerous man. So is McCann."

"My father and McCann were business partners for years!"

"*Ezra!*" The vehemence in her voice surprised her. It did Ezra, as well, who actually jumped a little in his seat. "I would not be here if I wanted to see you injured or worse. I have a great amount of information that you need to know." She hoped what she was about to say wasn't a lie, because she and Merritt still weren't completely certain if McCann or Penright murdered Ezra. "I know who killed your father."

The words worked as if by magic. Ezra's eyes widened for a few seconds. "Do you finally admit it?" he hissed.

"No, it wasn't me. I think I know who it was." She pointedly looked at his garden door. "May we go inside and I'll tell you everything?"

He rose and picked up his teacup. His shoulder

slumped a little in defeat. "Fine." He inclined his head to the door. "Come in, then."

She followed him through it, stepping into a tastefully appointed foyer. The entryway floor was finished with hundreds of tiny black and white tiles alternating with each other, a stark contrast to the deep green velvet paper gracing the walls. A brass chandelier topped with flameless candles dangled from the ceiling. An oil portrait of Edwin and his first wife, painted shortly after they were married, hung on the wall.

Ezra led her to the kitchen. Like the foyer, its colors were dark, muted. "Tea?"

He'd never offered her so much as a cup before. Her instincts went on alert and for the first time she questioned her visit. Was he going to poison her? What had Penright told him?

As if he could read her mind, he said, "It's unadulterated. I wouldn't be able to talk myself out of being hanged if you turned up dead."

"All right, then, I'd like a cup. Thank you."

He poured her cups for both of them from the brass pot on the polished wooden work surface. "Sit," he commanded, gesturing to the table. Two chairs were arranged on either side. Ivy took the closest one. "Do you mind if I smoke?" he asked.

She shook her head. "I thought you'd given that up."

He removed a box of matches and a flat silver case from his trousers pocket. He slipped out a cheroot and lit it. "Some habits take a while to break." He inhaled deeply, then took care to exhale away from Ivy. It was a small gesture, but she appreciated it. "Speak."

She wasn't sure where to start. "I'm not sure if you'll believe what I'm about to say."

"I've heard a great deal of unbelievable things over the

last couple of days. I'm certain nothing you could say would shock me at this point."

Was that why he was being almost hospitable to her? What had McCann and Penright told him, what powers had Penright demonstrated? Ivy doubted he knew that the medium killed Martha, otherwise he wouldn't be so calm. She was itching to tell that to Ezra, but knew she had to start at the beginning. "Your father and I didn't have a conventional marriage," she said.

"A man marrying a woman young enough to be his daughter is one of the most conventional events in Britain."

Ivy didn't rise to the bait. "I'm not young enough to be his child. His niece from an older sibling, perhaps."

Was it a trick of her imagination, or did Ezra bite back a smile at her reply?

"Your father sought me out for my healing abilities," she said. "I was working in an apothecary in Everton at the time."

"Yes, we all know how he walked into your little shop and fell head over heels for you."

There was the old Ezra emerging again. "He didn't fall head over heels for me, nor I for him. He'd had a series of terrible skin rashes and he couldn't figure out why they kept occurring. I made a poultice for him that cured him." She paused, unsure how to phrase the next part of her story. She'd repeated the lie about the poultice for years, and it felt so natural that she couldn't keep the words from leaving her. "No, it wasn't just the poultice. I cured his rashes with a spell, too."

Ezra stilled and stared at her.

Ivy waited for him to respond.

His eyes were blank, the expression a little unnerving.

She focused on the lazy curl of smoke that issued from the end of his cheroot. Finally, he said flatly, "A spell."

She nodded. "I'm a witch."

He leaned back in his seat and took a deep drag off the cheroot, followed by a swallow of tea. He looked away, gaze darting about the kitchen as if deciding what to look at. The only sound was that of a clock somewhere in the flat, ticking away the seconds. She wondered how he tolerated the noise at night.

A minute passed before he spoke. "Prove it."

She took that as an encouraging sign. "All right." She quickly uttered a quick spell that extinguished fires. The tiny ember at the end of Ezra's cheroot immediately went cold. He looked at it in surprise.

Ivy recited another spell, this one chilling the tea. Finally, she cast the last one, the spell that set light spilling from her hands, the same one she used in the bottling factory the night she and Merritt let themselves in.

Ezra stared at her glowing hands, expression still unreadable.

Ivy folded them together, breaking the spell. "I used my magic on the Miracle Elixir," she explained. "That's what makes it work so well. It's why your father married me, so I could have a controlling interest in the patent medicine that made him rich. Our marriage was a business arrangement, although we were friends."

Ezra relit his cheroot. "Friends."

At least he wasn't calling a constable or throwing her out of his flat. "Yes."

"And you're an honest to God witch."

"It runs in my family."

"You don't have a family."

"I have my sister."

He took a thoughtful puff off the cheroot. "If your family was healers and witches, why did they die?"

Was he trying to be cruel? "Magic can't fix everything. It can't fix old age or bodies after they've been caught under carriage wheels in the street. I can't resurrect people."

"Necromancers can."

A chill slid down Ivy's spine, resting at its base. "What? How do you know about necromancers?" A foolish question, since she already knew the answer and spoken Penright's name, but she wanted to hear what Ezra had to say.

Ezra stumbled over his next words. "People who claim to be necromancers say they can resurrect people."

"Some of them can, others just see and speak with the head. Like Merritt Sloan."

Ezra's brows lifted in surprise. "He's a necromancer?"

A measure of relief trickled through Ivy at his reaction. That had to mean that McCann and Penright didn't know what Merritt was, either. "That's how he excels in his work. He can ask murder victims exactly who killed them and how." He looked like he wanted to rely, but Ivy continued. "I know you've spoken to Roger McCann and he's introduced you to a medium named Penright."

"How…?"

"It's complex." It wasn't, but Ivy wasn't up to explaining the existence of vampires yet. "Penright murdered Martha. He mistook her for me."

Ezra froze. She thought she could see the breath freeze in his lungs. His gaze fixed on her, but she had the impression that he wasn't truly seeing her. His cheroot fell to the tiled floor. Ivy reached down to pick it up and dropped it in the brass ashtray on the table, wrinkling her nose at the smell. Finally, he said, "What?"

"Martha told Merritt the night she died. She met us outside before we even walked into the house. Her spirit did, anyway." Ivy's voice broke as the memory of that night hit her. "She couldn't stay long before being compelled to move on to whatever's beyond this plane."

"No." Ezra's face drained of color. "I've known Martha almost my entire life… why would he do that?"

"I told you! Penright wanted to kill me! That's why I had to leave the house, why I've been moving about from place to place since the night she died. He's after me next, on McCann's order. Roger McCann killed your father, Ezra, or ordered his murder, and Merritt and I are trying to prove it. With me out of the way, the full control of the company would be his!"

All Ezra could do was shake his head, an unreadable expression on his face.

"Penright captured your father's soul," Ivy continued. "We don't know how yet, nor how to free him. Merritt and I are working on that. This isn't just about money, this is about Edwin's afterlife. He deserves one."

Ezra didn't reply. The seconds ticked by on the clock, a sound that made Ivy want to pull off the device's hands. "What has to happen next?" he asked.

"What do you mean?"

He leaned forward, elbows resting on the table. "How do we get Penright out of the picture? Between you, Sloan, and me, there must be something we can do."

THE LIVERPOOL MUSEUM OF THE PARANORMAL was open to visitors, although there were few. Merritt was hardly surprised to see that at this relatively early hour, but he was certain that would change later in the day. Most ordinary people didn't think about ghosts at noon.

He paid his admission at an automaton installed at the front entrance. It was a large brass and glass box with an eerie mechanical head that nodded at him when he dropped coins into a copper box affixed to the front. Its blue-painted eyes blinked slowly and its rubbery lips lifted upward in a toothless smile that creaked. A shudder wracked through him. How had he not noticed it the other night? It was god-awful at best and ostentatious at worst.

Just as quickly, he answered his own question. He'd been too distracted by Ivy in her finery that evening. He was slipping as a private detective, letting himself be distracted to the point that he didn't notice a six-foot tall automaton at a museum's entrance.

The interior was still dark as it was the other night, its windows covered. The auditorium was closed and its door locked, with a painted sign on it that promised a reading by the Amazing Penright that very night. Another sign indicated where visitors should begin their self-guided tour, and Merritt followed its arrows down a corridor.

It was lit with electric lights, as were the glass-enclosed display cases holding objects alleged to be haunted. It was all a load of bollocks, as there wasn't a ghost to be found in the museum's main room, nor was anything supernatural attached to the collection of scarves and jewelry. Merritt wandered around, pretending to be interested in the made-up backstories of the collection that were printed on cards in front of each exhibit. He left the main exhibit room and peeked into a couple of other, smaller rooms, one of which was clearly set up for small séances. It was empty save for a round table covered with a black velvet cloth.

He opened an unmarked door to find a short, well-lit

corridor. A faint, muted hum greeted him, along with an odd, faint vibration that made his skin crawl. Nothing creepy festooned the bare walls. It looked like an ordinary office corridor, albeit a little rundown. There were closed doors on either side, also unmarked. Only the hum was unusual. Merritt's ears strained for other noises or voices, but heard nothing. Something odd was happening here, outside the usual weirdness one associated with the paranormal. An uneasy feeling settled in the pit of Merritt's stomach.

He knocked on the first door, then gently tried the knob. It opened easily, revealing a large closet filled with cleaning implements. He hastily closed it and knocked on the next door. This door revealed an empty, windowless office.

That left the door on the opposite side of the corridor. It turned out to be locked. He waited in front of it, debating the merits of breaking in and risking being injured by a protection spell, or leaving it as is and returning later with Ivy, who could unlock it with her own magic. It would be best to let himself in, he quickly decided. The sooner Penright was stopped, the sooner Ivy would be safe again.

He removed a ring of skeleton keys from his pocket. Working quickly, he was able to get the lock open. Merritt steeled himself, waiting for an explosion or horde of demons to suck the breath from his lungs, but nothing happened, except the hum grew louder. It sounded like the murmur of dozens of party guests crammed into a ballroom.

The room was dark, its drapes drawn tightly closed against the gray light outside. Merritt turned on an electric wall sconce affixed to the wall next to the door, sending dull yellow light across the small room. The desk was messy, stacked with papers, books, and pens but that wasn't what had Merritt nearly doubling back in shock.

The walls were lined with shelves, crammed with bottles and tubes. And each bore a label with the name of the soul trapped inside printed neatly in black ink, and every single one was begging Merritt to set them free.

THERE HADN'T BEEN time to look through the rows of bottles for Edwin Thaddeus's soul vessel. Horror and fury shot through Merritt's veins when he turned around and left Penright's office for the poor souls captured in them. He uttered a silent vow to himself, promising to return and free them. How the hell he would do that, he wasn't certain. Should he take a chance and break their vessels, or did the magic trapping them require another spell to let them loose?

He didn't run into any of the museum employees before he walked out of the building. His hands, thrust into his coat pockets, shook as he walked along the street. He scarcely noticed the light rain that misted around him as the morning turned into the afternoon while he walked back to his office. Fear and uncertainty wound through him when he thought about Ivy's visit with Ezra.

Not ten minutes after he returned to his office, Ivy let herself in, looking none the worse for wear. Before he could stop himself, he immediately reached for her and kissed her. She gasped against his lips but melted against him, immediately responding. "You're all right," he breathed against her mouth. His lips caught hers again before she could reply.

She pulled away, albeit reluctantly. "I told you Ezra wouldn't hurt me."

"How did the visit go?"

She hesitated. "I told him everything. He believed me. He… he invited us to a séance at McCann's house tomorrow night."

It took a few seconds for the weight of her words to hit him. "He did what?" Just as quickly, he recovered. "Are you certain that Ezra's reasons for doing so are honest?"

Ivy nodded. "Very. I told him everything: about what we are, Penright's relationship to McCann, Martha's murder. I demonstrated my magic, I told him about McCann's likely motivations for killing Edwin. The only thing I couldn't offer was how Edwin actually died."

"Magic?" Merritt offered.

"It must have been, or perhaps a poison that mimics heart failure. I'm not sure we'll ever know. Right now, the priority is freeing Edwin's soul from wherever it is."

Merritt's relief at seeing her safe in his office evaporated. He hated what he was going to have to tell her. "I visited the museum," he said.

Something in his voice told Ivy that what he'd discovered was serious. The color drained from her face. "Yes?"

"It didn't take long. Evidently, the demand for paranormal museums declines in the mornings." He was stalling. He wished he'd thought better how to tell her about the soul vessels. "I found an office that I suspect belongs to Penright. It was full of bottles and tubes, each one labeled with a different name." He searched for words to describe the sound. "They all hummed and vibrated. I think I found where Penright is holding souls."

Ivy held a hand to her mouth, eyes widened in shock and disgust. "Are you sure?"

"I could sense an odd presence when I was in there, as I got closer to the office. Multiple presences. It was the oddest sensation, like their voices were muted, as if they were calling to me from another room in a house. I think the office is too far away from the auditorium for me to have noticed the noise at the last séance."

"Why didn't you let them go while you were there?" Her voice caught. "Did you see Edwin's name?"

Shame tinged his words, even though he knew he'd done the responsible thing by not letting them out. "No, but I didn't look for him."

"They're captured souls, Merritt! Uncork the bottles!" Tears gathered in her eyes. "Why the hell didn't you let them go?"

"I didn't have time! I couldn't release dozens of souls all at once. Some of them could be violent. I have no idea of knowing which spirits are malevolent and which simply want to move on to the next world or which ones would need help to do so. I don't even know if opening the bottles would work!"

Ivy's voice rose in anger. "You could've freed some of them!"

"And risk Penright knowing the spirits are about and making things worse for them? No."

Ivy looked at him like she didn't believe him. The loss of her respect was palpable in that moment.

"I will free them," he promised her. "Very soon, after we've put Penright out of the way. It isn't safe for any of us until then."

Her lips quivered, then thinned. She nodded and looked away for a moment, looking around his office, as if truly noticing it for the first time. "I understand."

"I would have freed them then if I could."

"I know, and I apologize for snapping at you. Today was very emotional for me and Ezra."

Here he was, lusting after her, the wife of the dead man whose soul was likely enclosed in a glass tube in Penright's museum, calling out into the ether for years. "It's all right, Ivy. I'm not angry with you. I wish I could have done more back at the museum." The memory of their collective wailing, so many of them crying for freedom that it coalesced into that horrible hum, set his teeth on edge.

"I know you would have if it had been possible. I'm frustrated, is all. Appalled at the sheer greed of Roger McCann, grieving over Martha." She sighed and leaned against his desk, skirts rustling behind her. "Today was the first day that Ezra and I have ever had an honest conversation. It's the first time he's spoken to me like he didn't hate me."

"He had no reason to."

"He's loyal to his father. He was worried about Edwin and his marrying a much younger woman. I'm not angry with him. We've reached a truce." A small smile ghosted her lips. "Perhaps one day we can even be friends. He's offered me the use of his home tonight." Her gaze met his, color touching her cheeks. "I explained that we're both in danger and that Penright stopped by your flat last night. He's offered you the same."

Merritt inhaled sharply. "You told him about us?"

"You can't go back to your home. He knows where you live and we know what he's capable of. It isn't just about your safety, it's also about Claudia's."

She was correct about his ghostly flatmate. "Of course."

"Did you not want me to say anything about us?" she pressed. "Whatever we are?"

That begged the question of where their relationship stood. It was a hell of a time to start one with a widow in half-mourning, not that Merritt had much experience to measure that by. "No, it's not that. What did Ezra think of you, well, moving on?" Before she could answer, he continued, "Is that terribly insensitive of me to use those words?"

"No, it isn't. Edwin knew I would likely outlive him and would likely remarry." Remarry? An odd flare of an unfamiliar, but not unpleasant, feeling surged in him at the idea. Like Merritt's, her next words came out in a rush. "Not that I'm thinking about marriage and the like right now, I'm enjoying being with you even through all of this. Ezra gave us his blessing, although he did say he was surprised that you would take such unprofessional liberties given your reputation as a private detective." She grinned, the first happy expression she'd had since she arrived.

He couldn't keep himself from kissing her. "He sacked me, remember."

"He apologized for that. He says he'll tell you to your face the next time we see him."

"Ezra isn't worried about Penright appearing at his flat to murder all of us?"

She colored. "I didn't think to ask. Why would he? He has no idea that Ezra suspects him now."

Merritt filed away that answer, wanting to come back to it later. While Ivy seemed to be relieved at the possibility of a civil relationship with her stepson, Merritt didn't fully trust Ezra. He doubted the man would try to set them up in harm's way, now that he knew what McCann and Penright had done to his father, but he didn't believe that Ezra had the means to keep all of them safe. Perhaps it would be best if all of them spent the night away at yet another different location. "We could backtrack a little to throw him off. How safe would you feel returning to your house?" he asked.

"I wouldn't. Not until Penright is gone." Her voice was firm. "I don't think spending a night at Ezra's flat would harm us. It's the last place Penright or McCann would expect us to be. I can cast a protection spell around the flat that will alert me if anyone approaches. We can take watch in shifts if necessary, but I can't go back to the house until I know all of us will be safe."

"Are you prepared for the possibility that we'll have to kill someone?"

She nodded. "Ezra was ready to shoot both of them today. I had to talk him out of it."

So, Ezra was likely armed. That wasn't something that boded well for Merritt, who had seen all too often what could happen when anger trumped reason. They needed to keep McCann and Penright alive at least until they could be confronted. Merritt needed to know why they had acted the way they did, his compulsion to see a mystery solved, wouldn't let Ezra run off half-cocked and put bullets into the other men. Not to mention that Ezra himself would be hanged for such a crime. If McCann and Penright died at their hands, it would have to be of an untraceable cause unknown to humans.

"All right," said Merritt. He didn't like the idea, but it was the least-worst one they had right now. "We'll spend the night at Ezra's flat. We'll go before it gets dark out. We'll take my ornithopter." Flying through the city's air traffic wasn't ideal, but he didn't trust public transportation at the moment.

"Thank you." Some of the tension left Ivy's expression. Her shoulders relaxed. "All of this means a lot to me. I've only ever wanted to be on friendly terms with Ezra. I hope we can have that going forward."

Merritt understood her need for a familial connection. As overbearing as his parents could be, he loved them, couldn't imagine his life without them or his sister in it. When he thought of his parents, he thought of the unseelie fae spells. He and Ivy still hadn't had much of an opportunity to review and learn from. His face and body heated when he remembered what happened the last time they tried to study them. He ignored those feelings and tried to conjure up something more professional. Something in those old spells could prove useful. "Shall we look at the spells my mother gave us? At least the ones that Claudia said aren't for nuisance purposes?"

Ivy blinked, then her mouth twitched in a smile as she no doubt remembered what happened last time, too. "Yes, I suppose now is as good a time as any."

Merritt had locked the leather folder of foolscap in his desk drawer, wanting the thing to be as far away from him as possible. He removed it and put it on the scratched-up desk top, then flipped the cover open. The spells Claudia pointed out were on top, the words inked in a looping, left-handed scrawl. Resurrection spells, the kind of dark magic he'd sworn never to use.

Ivy picked up the foolscap, studying the words without speaking them. A line worried between her eyebrows as she concentrated, her expression shifting to one of disgust. "I could never do any of this."

"It's horrific. It's one thing to speak to a ghost who wants to see their murder prosecuted. It's another to force them into a body that's been violated or decomposing."

"I can't imagine. I don't want to." Ivy looked up. "I think I could cast these if I needed to. The words feel right. I'm not sure how to explain it."

Not having any fae magical abilities, Merritt's curiosity was piqued. "Try."

She lifted an eyebrow at his tone. "It's like having another sense. You can communicate with dead people. I can sense the magic in a spell. It's as natural as breathing for us. I think you should try and learn to cast this one."

"Absolutely not."

She crossed her arms over her chest. "Try."

Now it was his turn to give her an exasperated look her echoing his answer. "I've never cast a spell in my life."

"There's no time like the present to try. You already have the power to see and speak to the dead. It isn't unreasonable to assume you could cast a spell like your own ancestors did to bring their bodies back to life." She pointed at his wilting plants in the corner. "Resurrect that fern."

"I think it's beyond saving." The fern was brown, its soil dry. Merritt had stopped feeling guilty over his forgetting to water it weeks ago. He wasn't in his office often enough to remember to throw away the blasted thing.

"That's the point. It's dead and needs to be brought back to life for a time." She held out the spell to him, pressing the foolscap into his hand. "Say the words while pointing at the fern. We'll call it, uh, Percy. Percy Fern. You'll need a name to resurrect it."

Feeling ridiculous, Merritt sighed and gritted his teeth. He looked at the words and tried to make sense of the bizarre Latin-fae language. He sounded out the words, tongue stumbling over them. With his free hand, he touched the fern's desiccated leaves, willing them back to life. As he said the words, an odd electric current surged under his skin, as if he was gifting energy back to another being. Under the pads of his fingers, the texture of the leaves slowly changed, the color restoring itself to a shiny, healthy green.

Merritt stared at the plant in shock. "What the hell?"

Ivy beamed at him. "See? You can practice magic, after all."

"I'm not sure I want to." The eeriest sensation of power flowed through him, dark and demanding, an urge from his fae side. That small part of him wanted to do more, to wreak havoc on the human world for the hell of it the way his unseelie ancestors did. He closed his eyes and breathed deeply, willing away the feeling. "Ivy. I don't like this."

Her eyes widened in concern. "Not even a little?"

"No, I don't like having an ability to cast spells. I don't ever want to raise someone from the dead again. I don't like knowing I can do that. There's a part of me that wants to unleash hell across Liverpool." He glanced at the fern again. "How long will it stay alive?"

"I don't know. An hour or two, perhaps."

He shoved the spell back at her. His voice was hoarse to his ears, as if he'd just spent the last five minutes screaming. "I understand why this is important, but don't ask me to do that again." He shook his head, as if to dislodge the impulse to recite the words at a newly dug grave in St. James Cemetery just to see what would happen. The urge slowly pulsed away, like the fading of a life into a coma. He didn't know he was swaying on his feet until he nearly fell into Ivy, who steadied him.

"I didn't know," she whispered.

"It's all right. Neither did I." He forced himself to smile. "Now we know." He hated to see the distressed look on her face. He kissed her, putting everything in it that he could, to let her know he wasn't upset. Perhaps one day he would find this new skill useful.

She responded immediately, a moan of desire sounding low in her throat.

Merritt didn't think he could ever get tired of hearing

that. They wouldn't have any privacy soon, and he knew they would be facing a fight for their lives. A scandalous idea took hold. His fingers traced along the embroidered details of her coat collar, toying with one of its copper buttons. "Here," he murmured.

"What do you mean?"

"The door is locked." He inclined his head to it, its brass bolt in place. "But there are other tenants in the building, working. How quiet do you think you could be?"

A blush flamed in her cheeks. She smiled, a slow, sensual one that told him she liked the idea. "I can be quiet."

"And I'll try." He fastened his mouth over hers once more, hands reaching for her waist and meeting fistfuls of gray wool.

She broke the kiss to ask, "You don't make a habit of doing this in your office?"

He pulled away from her enough to meet her gaze. "Never. You're the only client I've ever done *anything* of this nature with. If I had any professional morals, I would have withdrawn from this case a long time ago."

She perched on the edge of the desk. An oddly serious expression settled on her face, at war with her eyes, now glazed with lust. "Why didn't you?"

He hadn't expected that. "Because I care about seeing the dead move on when they're ready and seeing murderers brought to justice. I care about you, more than anyone else." His need for her extended beyond conversation and bedsport. He wanted to know how she spent her days when she wasn't being hunted by a necromancer, how she liked to spend her holidays, whether she enjoyed flying or not. He wanted to wake up with her on lazy Sunday mornings and while away the hours with tea and the newspaper. He'd never wanted any of those things before.

"I don't know what this is," he continued, voice soft. "But I don't want it to end."

Something in her expression shifted slightly, became warmer, as if he'd broken down a wall neither of them knew she had erected. "Neither do I."

That was all the encouragement Merritt needed. He pushed up her skirts to caress her calf, bound in dark gray silk. A shiver wracked through her at the small touch. He grinned. This was going to be fun.

Awkward, but fun.

He gently urged her legs apart to stand between them. He could swear that he felt heat radiating off her even through their layers of clothes. Her hands locked around his head and brought him to hers for a kiss, tongue licking the seam of his mouth, demanding entrance. He was only too happy to grant it, the sensation sending sparks along his skin, setting every cell in his body at attention. He wished they had more time to explore each other, to spend time together without the specter of death hanging over their heads. That they weren't reduced to a quick, hurried coupling in his threadbare office, watched by a fern resurrected with dark fae magic.

Ivy's nimble fingers reached for his shirt buttons and unfastened them. There was a wicked gleam in her eye as she did, a promise he couldn't wait for her to keep. She slid off the desk and slowly lowered to her knees, eyes never leaving his face as she tugged at his trousers waistband, unbuttoning its placket.

Merritt's breath caught as he realized what she was about to do. He'd never dared to imagine such a thing ever happening to him in his workplace, let alone with someone like Ivy.

She pulled down his clothes enough to free him, her fingers stroking his length, already hard for wanting her.

She swiped her tongue over the head, a teasing gesture that had his muscles already tensing.

He wanted and needed so much more. "*Ivy*," he said through gritted teeth.

She gave him a wicked smile before taking him in her mouth.

The motion was almost Merritt's undoing. A strangled noise escaped her as she took him deeper, and he almost forgot his promise to be quiet. His hands found her hair, neatly arranged in a knot at the back of her head, and he silently urged her to continue. She hummed a little in the back of her throat, sending tiny vibrations echoing through him. His hips bucked against her, and he knew he would lose control far too quickly if she didn't stop.

Not yet. If he was going to do this with Ivy in his office of all places, he wanted it to be memorable. It took every ounce of his willpower to croak out, "Stop."

She did, looking up at him with wide eyes. "Why?"

"Get on the desk." He didn't try to hide the roughness in his voice.

She didn't waste a moment obeying. She perched on its edge. Merritt grabbed a handful of her skirts and pushed them up and out of the way. It was a shame she wasn't more undressed, but he supposed it was more practical. He reached for her drawers and rudely pulled them down, leaving them somewhere on the floor.

She bit back a moan when his fingers pressed against the wet well of her sex, eyes glazing over with desire.

Carefully, he lined himself up with her entrance, then surged forward.

Ivy cried out.

He caught her lips with his, muffling the noise as he withdrew and thrust into her again. Her fingers dug into his shoulders, nails scraping him through his shirt's fabric as he repeated it over and over until a keening cry began to rise in her throat. "Quiet," he reminded her, his voice a murmur in her ear.

Ivy's only response was to bite him as her orgasm ripped through her.

He would have grinned at her reaction, but his own crested on him, sooner than he wanted. Not being vocal as he came proved to be the most difficult impulse to overcome in his life, more than the lure of unseelie magic ever did. It was another miracle from the gods that his legs didn't give out beneath him as the shudders wracked him. He didn't move, not wanting to leave the warm depths of Ivy's body before he had to. He pressed a kiss to her neck as he tried to catch his breath. He could swear their hearts beat in tandem for a few seconds.

He wasn't sure how much time passed before Ivy said, "Will that tide you over?"

"Mm?" He was still inside her, half-leaning over the desk.

"Until we can spend a weekend in bed, safely. Will that tide you over?"

"No." He may as well be honest. Ivy had become precious of him in a way no one else ever had, in a very short expanse of time. "I don't think I'll ever be satisfied as long as I'm not with you."

# CHAPTER 16

Ivy rarely had cause to visit Ezra, and she hadn't seen much of his flat until that day. It was a beautifully appointed space, she noted, filled with the latest in modern technology. She couldn't stop to admire it for the anxiety filling her.

Ezra showed her and Merritt to his spare bedroom. "My apologies for the cleaning," he said stiffly. "My housekeeper wasn't in today and I had to do it myself."

The room looked fine by Ivy's standards, although it smelled a little dusty, overlaid \with furniture polish. "This is all right. We appreciate your hospitality."

"Well, I want to see this over with as soon as possible." Ezra looked away for a moment, blinking at his reflection in the looking glass against the blue-papered wall. At that moment, Ivy thought he looked younger than the twenty-seven years she knew him to be. She saw him as the young man still grieving over his mother's death, who watched his father marry a woman young enough to be his sister with hardly an explanation as to why. She and Ezra still had much to talk about.

Her stepson was all business after she and Merritt left their bags in their room. They'd hurried back to his flat to change their clothes and collect their things after their interlude in his office, a memory that brought a fierce heat to her face. She brushed it aside as she padded through the flat, feeling out of sorts in Ezra's space. It wasn't welcoming like her home or Merritt's. It felt cold, almost as if it was a museum that no one lived in. Save for a couple of framed photographs and an oil painting of his parents, there was little in the way of personal touches.

She found Ezra in his parlor, nursing a glass of whiskey. "Merritt was in his cups the first time we spoke outside the house," she said by way of greeting.

Ezra's voice was steady, not one of someone who had had too much to drink. "Where is he now?"

"In our room, teaching himself unseelie fae spells in case he needs them tomorrow."

Ezra shook his head. "Fae and a necromancer. Hell of a thing to be."

"He's mostly human," she protested. "He resurrected a fern in his office today."

"Is that good? I have no measure by which to judge that."

"He wasn't sure he could resurrect anything anymore, so I suppose so."

"Why can't you cast the spells? You're a witch."

"My magic doesn't work like that."

"There are different types of magic?" He sounded genuinely curious instead of disdainful. It was a refreshing change.

"Yes, but I don't know a lot of other people with these abilities. Witch magic can be practiced by witches, fae magic by fae, and so on."

Ezra inclined his head at the bottle of whiskey on the sideboard. "Do you want some?"

"Yes." Drinking might make this conversation easier to bear.

"Help yourself."

She did, pouring a healthy measure into a glass. Ivy took a seat on a chair opposite Ezra, who was carelessly sprawled out across his settee. "Speaking of fae magic, tomorrow night is going to be very dangerous," she said.

"I supposed it would be." Despite the flippancy of his words, she heard an undercurrent of nervousness there. He was scared. He was right to be.

She was, too. "I don't know how to prepare." She may as well be honest.

"What did you have planned with Merritt?"

"Killing Penright and releasing the souls he's captured."

"I'll kill Penright." The trace of fear in his voice was gone, his bravado bolstered by his need for vengeance for Edwin. "Let me do it."

"Roger McCann will be there, too."

"I'll kill him, too. Sloan would know how to help me get rid of the bodies."

A chill slithered down Ivy's spine at his vehemence. This was the Ezra she was familiar with: cocksure, arrogant, determined to see things through his way at whatever cost, but amplified. "Penright is a very dangerous man," she reiterated.

"I don't care. He's stolen my father's soul. He deserves to die for that." He straightened and set his empty glass on the table. "I'll be armed tomorrow night."

"Where the hell did you get a weapon?"

"It's a clockwork pistol."

"That doesn't answer my question."

"You're not my mother." He said the words without a trace of malice and leaned back against the sofa's cushions.

Ivy thought he might actually be teasing her for the first time. She wasn't in a teasing mood. "I know," she replied quietly. "I never tried to be your mother."

"I did appreciate that, even if I haven't told you until today." He hesitated, choosing his words carefully. "I don't hate you, Ivy. I never have."

"Are you certain of that?"

He looked at her, a sheepish expression on his face. "I thought I did for a while. I thought you married my father for his money."

She didn't rehash the details about her marriage to his father now. He was talking to her, being open. She didn't want to interrupt him and cause him to withdraw again.

"I knew, deep down, that you didn't kill my father. It was just easier to blame you. I'm sorry, Ivy. I'm sorry for all the trouble I've caused and for not leaving you be in the house. I don't want it, I never have. It hasn't been my home since my mother died."

"The house is too big for me on my own, anyway. I've thought of selling it."

"It's still your house. You loved it there. Father left it to you when he knew I didn't want to stay."

"It's been forever tainted by Martha's murder. I don't think I want to live there again."

"I'm truly sorry about Martha. And I'm sorry for bringing all of this on you and Sloan." He cleared his throat. "You couldn't even wait until you were out of mourning?"

"Ezra…"

"I'm being an ass. I don't care that you've taken up with Sloan. You have heaps more in common with him than Father."

"Your father and I cared about his patent medicine and keeping it available in its original form, with my magic. I couldn't have asked for a better partner."

"It's different with Sloan. I could tell from the first time I met him at the house, the way he looked at you. I don't think you noticed."

An odd feeling settled in the pit of her stomach, a curious mix of elation and embarrassment. "I don't know what to say."

"You don't have to say anything," Ezra insisted. "I'm not angry with you, or Sloan for that matter. I wish you and Father had thought to tell me about your abilities before he died. It would have cleared a lot of the air."

"That wasn't my call to make."

"I know, but Father still should have told me. It's a hell of a thing to find out your father's business partner may have had him killed, then hired a necromancer to steal his soul for whatever ghastly reason, *and* find out that your stepmother is a witch. I've had a lot to take in today. It's going to take a while." He drained his glass and set it on the table in front of him with a thump. "Can you turn water into wine?"

She hadn't been expecting that. "What? No. I'm not Jesus."

He shrugged. "Thought I'd ask. What about alchemy?"

"I suppose I could cast a spell that would make something take on the appearance of gold for a time, but I couldn't change its structure. My magic is mostly domestic. I'm a healer."

"So was Jesus," he replied dryly.

Perhaps it was the exhaustion pulling at her, the near-constant urge of fighting or fleeing she'd experienced since all of this started, but she found his flip answer hilarious.

"I'm not sacrificing myself and rising again on the third day."

He looked amused at her reaction. "Why not? Sloan could resurrect you."

"I'm not so sure about that, he's only managed to resurrect a fern. Humans are a bit more complicated, I'm sure." She finished her drink, savoring its burn down her throat.

He didn't reply for a moment, instead staring at an oil painting depicting a crumbling castle in a field on the opposite side of the room. When he did, all traces of mirth had vanished from his voice. "If we get through tomorrow alive, I'd like it if we could be friends, Ivy."

"We will." She hoped he didn't notice the tremor in her voice. She was terrified of what they would face tomorrow night. "Somehow, we'll get through this."

MERRITT LINGERED OVER THE SPELLS, reading and re-reading them even though he'd already memorized them. The words were meaningless to him, but he could sense their dark power, could feel the allure the unseelie fae would have had when they still existed. It was a heady, frightening feeling, to know that he might not be able to trust himself around this magic if he had to be around it any longer than necessary.

Humans were so much safer.

He heard the murmur of voices in Ezra's parlor and stayed away. He wanted to give him and Ivy privacy. His ears strained to hear any sharp words or yelling, but none came. Ivy returned to their room shortly before supper time, cheeks flushed with the telltale sign of too much whiskey but she wasn't upset. "Ezra's sent out for supper. It will be delivered in an hour." She peered in the room's looking glass. "I'll need a nap before then."

Merritt moved over on the bed where he'd been poring over the spells. "I'll wake you when supper is ready."

She collapsed in a pile of skirts on the bed, then rolled over on her side to face him. "We need a better plan for tomorrow night. Ezra's promised to bring his gun. I didn't even know he owned one."

An inexperienced marksman fueled by rage would only make things worse. "I'll carry the gun in that case, if it will put your mind at ease."

"Nothing about this will ever put my mind at ease." Her voice wavered. She levered herself up on one elbow, better to face him. "You're too important to me to get hurt or worse."

His heart skipped a beat at her words. She was important to him, in a way he'd never felt for anyone before. He desperately wanted to promise her that everything would go without a hitch, but he didn't want to lie to her. She wouldn't believe him, anyway. "I will try very hard to keep all of us alive tomorrow."

"I know you will."

He pressed a kiss to her forehead. "Get some sleep."

She snuggled deeper into the pillow. "I'll try."

Merritt turned down the lamp and left the room, closing the door behind him. He found Ezra in his garden, smoking a cheroot while staring glumly at the street. Without turning around, Ezra said, "I don't suppose it's too dangerous for us to be outside at the moment?"

"I don't know. I don't think our staying inside would stop Penright if he wanted to get to us." Merritt sat in the iron chair next to Ezra. "Ivy tells me you're armed."

"Not at the moment, but I have a clockwork pistol in my bedroom."

"I'll take that tomorrow." Ezra opened his mouth to protest, but Merritt continued. "I know what I'm doing with a weapon while under pressure."

"I don't want to feel useless."

"You won't be. You've agreed to help us and started to clear the air with Ivy. She's wanted that for a long time."

Ezra exhaled cheroot smoke. "My relationship with Ivy is very complicated. I'm certain she's already told you."

"She has, and that's between you two. I want to speak with you about the séance tomorrow night. It's very important that we form a plan together, and everyone takes part in it according to their skills." Now it was Merritt's turn to feel nervous and hear a waver in his voice. "I have to use magic I'm unfamiliar with and hope it works, but not *too* well, since I could kill someone who doesn't deserve to be killed or raise an undead army, I'm not sure. Working with fae magic is unsettling."

"Ivy mentioned you're something to that effect."

"It's from a few generations back. It accounts for why I and my parents can see and speak to the dead. An unseelie fae could shapeshift at will and raise the dead too."

"And they can't now?"

"Unseelie fae don't exist anymore. They scattered, mated with seelie fae and humans alike, centuries ago." Merritt sighed. "I suppose dying out was their one true contribution to bettering humanity."

"You can't fly, don't have wings?"

Hadn't Ben Lang shared the same curiosity? Why the hell did everyone keep asking him if he had wings? "No."

"Do you know any species who can?"

Merritt hesitated. "Some vampires can." The vampire he knew wasn't very good at it.

Ezra stared at him. "Fuck me, they're real, too?"

Merritt nodded.

"Huh. I suppose werewolves are, too."

"Possibly. Mermaids definitely are, although I haven't met one yet. I found a laboratory at the Albert Dock that I suspected housed one, a couple of years ago." He tried to steer the conversation back to the séance. "About tomorrow night…"

"There was a *mermaid* in Liverpool?"

"Ezra, we really should discuss what happens tomorrow."

"Mermaids and vampires." Ezra blinked and took a final pull off his cheroot. He stubbed it out in a heavy brass ashtray half-filled with smoked cheroots. "My stepmother is a witch and my father believed in the paranormal. I've learned a lot today."

"To be fair, the paranormal is real. Legends and myths wouldn't exist without at least a trace of truth to them. Ivy and I will be happy to tell you everything we know, after tomorrow night."

"Fine." Ezra reached for his silver cheroot case and flipped open its lid to find it empty. He tossed it aside, irritated. Merritt was secretly pleased. The smell was abominable, even outside. "I promise I will not shoot anyone on sight tomorrow."

"You'll behave as normal, or as normal as you can at a séance."

"I'm unsure of the etiquette."

"Wear somber colors and pretend that the table knocking isn't being done by the medium or his assistant."

"Then, you confront him."

"We'll do that together. We'll have Penright and McCann in the same room together to answer your questions." Now that he spoke the words aloud, Merritt didn't feel as discombobulated about the séance. He'd been in dangerous situations with supernatural creatures more unhinged than Penright before. His primary concern now was the possibility of having to use unseelie fae magic.

"We'll take them by surprise," Ezra said, although he still didn't look convinced. "We still have to speak with Ivy."

"She's napping until supper. It seems she had a little too much whiskey."

"Both of us did." Ezra barely suppressed a yawn. "A little bit made the conversation that much easier for us."

"I'm glad you're making peace with her. She doesn't have any other family other than her sister."

"Neither do I, aside from a great aunt on my mother's side." His voice caught. "I wish she and Father told me everything sooner. We could have been friends."

Merritt hadn't deeply considered the late Dr. Thaddeus's silence on the reasons for his second marriage, and he should have. Edwin should have trusted Ezra with his and Ivy's secrets, should have treated him as an equal when he entered adulthood. Keeping mum on it had only ruined his relationship with his son. If Ezra had known about them and the reason for the Miracle Elixir's popularity, he might have tried with Ivy to keep the company running the way Dr. Thaddeus always intended. Perhaps his father's soul wouldn't have been stolen. No, Merritt chastised himself. It was important not to think like that, not to assign blame to an innocent party.

Ezra removed his silver watch from his pocket and checked the time. He put his empty cheroot case into another pocket. "Supper will be delivered shortly."

"I'll wake Ivy."

"Let her sleep until it arrives. I'll set the table." Something in Merritt's expression must have unsettled Ezra, because he added, "I'm perfectly capable of setting a table and clearing up when my housekeeper isn't in. I'm a bachelor, not an overgrown child."

"Understood. I'm of the same stock."

Ezra held open the door for him. "Are you certain of that? I doubt you'll remain a bachelor forever."

It took a few seconds for the weight of his words to sink in. The odd feeling that spread through him when he thought about Ivy and a future with her returned, bright as a full moon.

# CHAPTER 17

THE FOLLOWING EVENING, the three of them left Ezra's flat for Roger McCann's home in Woolton. They took Merritt's ornithopter to a small public flight station near McCann's address to secure it, wanting to have their own means of escape or even body transport later that night. Ezra looked distinctly green while the ornithopter was in the air. Ivy tried to give him a reassuring look, but knew it would be false.

She was *terrified* about the night ahead.

Confront McCann and Penright, then take action. She repeated the plan to herself over and over, as if that could soothe her. Find out what their motivations were, take steps to reverse the spells on all of the souls Penright had taken, find out *why* he'd done the horrific things he had. Part of Ivy thought it was nonsense to waste time on finding out the whys, but Merritt pointed out the necessity of knowing a villain's motivation to help unravel their mysteries. She supposed it was his detective experience that had him working along those lines.

They took a steam cab to McCann's home, a nicer

vehicle than the ones clattering through Merritt's neighborhood and the city center. McCann's house was palatial, a new money monstrosity with mismatched towers on either side of it that reminded Ivy of an ugly dollhouse. Reproduction Corinthian columns lined the front of the house and a set of marble steps led to the front door. Its circular drive was constructed of pink and black granite that sparkled under electric lights set on tall lamp posts. The front garden was filled with raised beds that were covered with burlap in anticipation of the winter, not unlike the gardens at Ivy's home. That was where the similarities in their houses ended.

The lights on the lower floor were ablaze through the windows. A couple of steam-powered vehicles waited in the drive, their driver's boxes empty. The three of them paused at the street, each gathering their courage in their own way to walk up the granite stones and knock on the door. "You've remembered all your spells, haven't you?" Ezra murmured.

"Of course." Merritt's voice was steady. Ivy was grateful to hear that strength. They might get through this alive and with their souls intact yet.

"And my gun?" Ezra had a slight emphasis on the word "my."

Despite her fear, Ivy bit back a smile.

"On my person and loaded."

"Let's go." Ezra started for the front door, then halted when he saw Ivy and Merritt weren't following. "Well?"

To Merritt, Ivy said quietly, "I want to kiss you for luck, but I don't know if we're being watched." How would it look to her husband's business partner if she was kissing someone else while she was still in half-mourning? Her black lace-trimmed gray skirts and jacket screamed her status to anyone passing by.

"You can kiss me all you like when we've finished this unpleasant business." The look Merritt gave her was full of promise. Ivy shivered in a way that had nothing to do with the night ahead. He nodded at Ezra and followed him up the drive, Ivy trailing behind.

Ezra rang the doorbell and a discordant chime clanged through the house, loud enough to be heard on the porch, loud enough to wake the dead. Ivy cringed at the idea, then schooled her features into a neutral expression when the door was opened by a dour-faced butler in his sixties. "Mr. Thaddeus," the butler murmured, holding it open for him.

"Peters," Ezra replied in greeting. "This is Mrs. Thaddeus, my father's widow, and our friend, Mr. Merritt Sloan, private detective."

He gave a slight nod, a picture of propriety. "Mr. McCann is waiting for you in the grand parlor. Allow me to take your coats."

Ivy let Peters remove her gray overcoat. Merritt did likewise, and Ivy noticed the slight bulge at his back where he'd hidden Ezra's clockwork pistol. How would he get to it in an emergency? She took a deep breath and reminded herself that he knew what he was doing with weaponry.

Peters led them through the house, its decorations as gaudy and ostentatious as its exterior. The walls were covered with flocked velvet paper, the carpets plush underneath their feet. Modern artwork graced the walls, the pieces chosen and arranged with little cohesion. The rooms they passed were filled with expensive-looking furniture made of heavy dark wood, their brocaded cushions overstuffed. Brass and copper sculptures appeared every few feet on slender plinths, all vaguely human-shaped. The house felt close and suffocating.

Peters led them into a back parlor, its red velvet walls

an assault on good taste. A shiny black-lacquered cabinet rested against the opposite wall, matching the black chairs and tables scattered around the room. There were more twisted metal sculptures here, causing Ivy to wonder if Roger McCann bought them at a bulk discount. A round table was in the middle of the room, draped with a black velvet cloth that reached the floor. A pair of squat black candles rested on it, dripping wax into their brass holders.

Ivy wasn't superstitious and didn't hold a lot of regard for candle colors in spells, but for some reason, the choice of black for tonight's candles felt… off. A threat. The room itself felt strange, like a light electrical current buzzed through it. She was in the presence of a magic practitioner, one with abilities she hadn't heard of before. What the hell was Penright, other than a medium?

McCann let himself into the room via another door on the opposite wall, next to the cabinet. She wondered where it led. He blinked in surprise at the sight of her. "Mrs. Thaddeus."

"Hello, Mr. McCann. Ezra invited us along tonight." She nodded at Merritt, who gave her a small smile. She relaxed a little. "You remember Detective Sloan?"

McCann blinked owlishly behind his spectacles and didn't respond for a few seconds. "Yes, of course. Good to see you again, Detective. I'm surprised you'd agree to accompany young Ezra tonight."

"We've embarked on a friendlier relationship."

"I'm surprised that a man of your profession would stoop to attending a séance. The paranormal is an interest of mine, as it was for the late Dr. Thaddeus, too."

"Part of being a good detective is broadening one's experiences and mind," Merritt replied coolly.

McCann blinked again. "Of course. Please take seats. Mr. Penright is preparing." To Ivy and Merritt, he asked,

"Have you heard of Mr. Penright? His abilities to contact the dead are quite extraordinary."

"I've heard of him," Merritt replied. His gaze was dragged somewhere in the corner of the room. Ivy wondered if he was seeing a ghost and if so, what it was telling him.

"I spoke to Ezra about arranging a meeting of this kind to speak to his father." Something flashed in his expression, dark and ugly. McCann pinned Ivy with a hard stare. She fought the urge to shudder. He'd never looked at her with hatred before. Bewilderment, perhaps, when she married Edwin. Exasperation when she started participating in the making of the Miracle Elixir, but never outright loathing. Just as quickly, it was gone, and McCann's expression relaxed.

Ivy didn't. "I'm not sure Edwin would appreciate being disturbed this way."

McCann's reply had an edge to it that chilled her blood. "I'm unsure Edwin wanted the company to take the direction you've insisted on taking it, nor is Ezra."

Ivy and Ezra exchanged quick glances. Ezra shook his head. "Father didn't leave the company to me. He knew I had no interest in taking it over. I haven't the head for numbers or business."

"Yet you've been so angry about your stepmother being left the bulk of Edwin's estate."

"She was left the family home and the company. Most of the liquid assets were willed to me. You know that."

McCann regarded Ezra thoughtfully for a moment, head tilted to the side. "I'm surprised, Ezra. The last time we spoke, you were quite eager to see your stepmother out of the picture."

Ivy's knees went weak. Was she wrong about Ezra? Had he pretended to care about her only to lure her here tonight? She swayed on her feet, steadied by Merritt's hand at her back.

"I said nothing of the sort," Ezra said sharply. "I had some serious reservations about Ivy's intentions with my father when they were married and her motivations. We've had a chance to talk about that and we've come to an understanding."

Ivy could have cried from relief. She and Ezra were still on the same team.

"I agreed to come here tonight to speak to my father on the advice of your medium friend," Ezra continued. "I brought Ivy here because she was curious. So was Detective Sloan."

"Ah, yes, the private detective you hired to prove your stepmother killed your father. Why the hell are you still bothering with him?"

"We've become friends, and he was curious, too." Ezra looked at the doors leading to the room, in front and behind them. "Where is this medium?"

"Meditating in the back garden. He has to do that before each séance."

Or he wanted to skulk about outside a room to learn about the séance attendees and gather information to appear authentic. Ivy made a mental note to ask Merritt about that later.

Peters entered the room through the same doorway McCann used. "Mr. Penright has finished his meditation and says the spirits are waiting." He sounded like he couldn't believe the words he was saying.

Ivy didn't, either.

"Excellent. Send him in, all of our guests have arrived." McCann took a seat at the round table. Ivy took one opposite him, and Ezra took the seat between her and McCann. So it would be Merritt sitting next to the medium himself. Ivy found that reassuring and worrying at the same time. She cared about him too much to see him hurt or worse.

Merritt caught her eye, and despite the palpable tension in the room, winked at her.

Even in a situation as dangerous as this, her heart managed to do a silly little flip-flop. More than caring. He had become more important to her than anyone else ever had, in a short period of time. If they came out of tonight's séance alive and well, their souls intact, she wanted to stay at his side. Ivy had never been in love before, but she thought she might be falling into it. Hell of a time to realize that. She suddenly wished she'd talked about that with him before tonight.

Peters left the room without another word.

Ivy was grateful to be sitting; she wasn't sure her legs could support her in that moment. She caught Ezra's expression, but it was unreadable. Her mouth went dry. She was about to meet the man who murdered Martha, who might have murdered her husband.

Penright swept into the room a moment later like a gust of cold air, black robe billowing out from behind him. "Good evening," he announced. "Roger, thank you for hosting me tonight. Mr. Thaddeus, a pleasure to see you again."

"Hello, Mr. Penright." Ezra nodded at Ivy and Merritt. "I brought my stepmother and father's widow, Mrs. Thaddeus with us this evening, and our friend, Detective Merritt Sloan."

Ivy scarcely heard Ezra's introductions. Penright stared at her and Sloan with a look of revulsion that was ten times greater than McCann's earlier in the evening. "Hello," Ivy squeaked.

Penright's mouth twisted into a scowl.

She had the distinct impression that he knew exactly who she and Merritt were and why they were there. She thought she might be sick.

They'd made a mistake coming here tonight.

Penright sat at the table in the last chair, between McCann and Merritt. "We're here to summon the spirit of one Dr. Edwin Thaddeus," he announced. "A man whose soul has been wandering since his untimely death, waiting to speak his final words."

A man whose soul he had stolen, possibly secreted away in a glass bottle. Rage swelled in Ivy, overriding her terror of the man.

"A man who was taken by the affections of no one but a common witch." Penright pinned Ivy with a stare.

She thought she might be sick. She resisted the urge to fidget or flee, even though every sense told her to run. This wasn't going according to plan. They were supposed to take him by surprise. He wasn't supposed to know she was a witch.

Hoping he was actually speaking of her being bewitching in the figurative sense, Ivy said, "I don't have a clue what you're speaking about. I'm here to find out if you can really speak to my husband."

Merritt's hand reached for hers and squeezed it, a motion that didn't go unnoticed by the others at the table.

Her breath caught.

"All right." Penright leaned back. "Everyone, join hands. Detective Sloan, I see you've done that already."

Ivy hated that Merritt would have to touch Penright. Her skin crawled at the idea of it.

All of them did so, then Penright began to chant, ordering spirits to appear the same way he did in his museum. It didn't feel the same in McCann's house: the air changed, grew thicker and harder to breathe. The table vibrated under them, and something clattered in the black-lacquered cabinet. If Ivy didn't know any better, she would have sworn that the room was full of ghosts. Perhaps it was.

"Show yourself!" Penright shouted. A painting fell off the wall.

Ivy squealed in fright.

"Fuck," muttered Merritt.

One of the brass sculptures fell over, the noise causing Ezra to jump in his seat. Penright's voice changed, became lyrical, then began to chant in Latin. There was something off about the words, as if someone had heard Latin a time or two and then constructed their own version of it.

"Oh, my God," she said aloud.

It was the language of the unseelie fae, the same dark magic wielded by Merritt's ancestors hundreds of years ago. The same spells that brought chaos to humans and meddled with their dead.

Without ceasing his chanting—no, *casting*, Ivy corrected herself—Penright let go of Merritt's hand and reached into his pocket. He set an ordinary glass bottle on the table.

Ivy's stomach turned over. "Edwin!" she cried.

Ezra let go of her hand and McCann's. "Father!"

Penright didn't answer, instead raising his voice. Merritt sprang out of his seat and reached for his back, withdrawing the clockwork pistol. McCann yelped when he saw the weapon and stood up from his seat. In that moment, the bottle cracked. Silvery steam issued from it, floating to Penright's side and coalescing into human shape.

"Why couldn't you leave him alone?" Ezra bellowed. "Why have you taken his soul?" Without another provocation, he leapt across the table at Penright, wrapping his hands around the medium's throat and knocking him out of his chair.

All hell broke loose.

McCann was out of his chair in a heartbeat, trying and failing to remove Ezra from beating the shit out of Penright. Ivy picked up the toppled brass statue when McCann reached for her, then swung it to keep him away from her. "I know you did it," she said through her tears. "I just want to know *how* you killed Edwin."

He reached for the other end of the statue and pulled it, nearly knocking her off balance. "Hemlock."

She sobbed and pulled the statue back, out of his hands, then swung it again. It connected with his hip.

He cried out and fell against the cabinet.

"Why?"

He winced in pain. "He left everything to you. *You*! He refused to innovate! He deserved to be punished for all of that!"

He had refused to poison his customers, he meant. Edwin had steadfastly refused to change the Miracle Elixir's formula, relying on its old-fashioned recipe of herbs and plants, enhanced by Ivy's magic. "He trusted you!" Behind her, she heard shouts and grunts as Ezra and Penright were locked in a bitter fistfight. It wasn't until a woman's scream ripped through the air that every person in the room came to a standstill to look at the source.

"Claudia?" Merritt's voice was preternaturally calm, as if he couldn't believe what he was seeing.

The woman screamed again. She swayed on her feet next to the table, wearing an odd, old-fashioned brown wool garment that reminded Ivy of a toga. Her midnight-black hair was woven in a neat braid, her color high on her tanned face.

"Step out of the way, Claudia," said Merritt, weapon cocked and aimed squarely at Penright.

THE GHOST of Roger McCann's wife had started talking at him as soon as he entered the house, ordering him to put an end to this nonsense and send her back to the afterlife. Merritt had every intention of doing so, as soon as this unpleasant business was over with.

He had to tune out the Mrs. McCann's ghost while he focused on the living woman in front of him who had been a spirit herself not an hour ago. How the hell was Claudia here, alive and breathing? What had Penright done to her? He thought the other necromancer had Dr. Thaddeus's spirit in that tube, not Claudia. She rushed to the nearest wall to stay out of the fray, not knowing where else to go. She stumbled on her legs, undoubtedly unused to having limbs after being a ghost for centuries. Claudia's breath came noisily, as if she was drowning trying to breathe air. His heart lurched at not being able to immediately help her.

Penright finally gained the upper hand while fighting with Ezra, shoving him aside and rising to face Merritt. Ezra landed at Claudia's feet, his nose bloody, and stared up at her in shock. With one hand on the wall, she held out the other to help him up.

The medium launched himself at Merritt. Merritt remained steady on his feet, then delivered a punch to Penright's jaw. "Why are you doing this?" he said through gritted teeth.

"You're unseelie, the same as I am." Penright grabbed Merritt's wrist, the hand that held his weapon.

Merritt twisted it out of the way, wincing at the pain as he did so.

"How the hell do you know that?" Out of the corner of his eye, he saw McCann creep toward them. Merritt wrenched himself out of Penright's grasp and raised his clockwork pistol again, squarely at McCann's chest. "This isn't a warning."

McCann closed the short distance between them and tried to knock the weapon out of his hand.

Merritt fired. His aim was a little off.

A bullet lodged itself in the cabinet. Ivy and Claudia screamed, McCann stumbled back, unharmed but shaken up.

Merritt's ears rang, which was irritating, but that meant everyone else's ears had to be, too. He took advantage of it by pushing Penright against the table, then pressed the barrel of his gun under the man's throat. "How did you know about me?" he said, although he could hardly hear himself.

He had to read Penright's lips as the other man replied. "The ghosts told me the night you visited my museum. I already suspected as much, though. No mere police consultant or detective could have solved as many murders as you did with as little evidence as you had without some kind of supernatural help." He squirmed against Merritt's hold, but Merritt only tightened his grip on his throat. "Why haven't you tried to live as the fae did?"

"Is that why you've stolen all of those souls? For fae magic?"

"It's necessary for unseelie magic. Your ghost friend is the first person I've successfully resurrected without a body to return to." Despite the grave danger he was in with a gun under his neck, Penright still managed to look smug. "She was easier to catch than I thought she would be."

"You had no fucking right. Not to her or any of the others."

"They're *humans*, Sloan."

"So are we!"

"No, we're something better than humans. Better than *witches*." He nearly spat out the word. "The unseelie deserve to rise again, to take their place as the head of the human hierarchy."

"They had their own court!"

"A court held over humans. We can assemble such a court again. I know the power to raise the dead is inside you. Embrace it." Penright's eyes nearly glowed. He began to chant again in the dead fae language, a spell Merritt was unfamiliar with.

He could sense its power, though, could feel what it was meant to do. The breath escaped his throat and his body started to go limp. He could feel each of his functions start to shut down as the ghastly spell Penright cast sucked the life from him. Dimly, he was aware of his grip loosening, the pistol hitting the carpet, as he collapsed to his knees. He felt the light start to leach from his eyes, could only dimly make out Ivy's shape as she rushed to him, screaming his name.

He tried to form words, tried to tell her he loved her, but nothing would come as he sank to the floor.

# CHAPTER 18

THE ROOM once again exploded into pandemonium. Ivy screamed as Merritt collapsed to the carpeted floor, a dazed look on his face as Penright continued to chant.

McCann looked confused, unsure whether to help the medium or throttle her.

Claudia… the poor girl could barely stand as she took in the sight before her.

Ezra sprang to his feet and grabbed the clockwork pistol. He caught Ivy's eye for half a second as he cocked it. Not knowing what else to do, she reached Merritt's side, bending down to hold him as Penright continued his hideous spell.

Another gunshot rent the air. The chanting stopped. Penright wavered on his feet for a couple of seconds, as if he held himself upright by pure spite, before he fell back on the table, then crashed facedown to the floor.

Ivy's ears hadn't stopped ringing since the first time the gun was fired, and it only got worse now. She cradled Merritt's head in her lap. "Wake up," she urged him, though she couldn't hear herself. "Wake up!" His head lolled to the side, but he sputtered, then coughed. "Oh, thank the gods!"

Someone shook her shoulder. Claudia now sat next to her, and she pointed at Ezra. He was still on his feet, pistol aimed squarely at McCann. The older man held his hands up in a gesture of defeat, but Ezra didn't waver.

The door Penright used opened a crack, and the confused face of Peters the butler appeared through it. Ivy couldn't hear what he was saying, but McCann's face went ashen and he lowered it. Ezra didn't move.

What the hell was happening?

Merritt hauled himself to a seated position, then gripping the table, to his feet. The ringing in her ears started to subside, and she could hear him speak to McCann. "You poisoned your business partner with hemlock," he announced. "That's a hanging crime in this country."

"Only if it can be proven."

"I'm certain we'll find proof of it somewhere and then you offered his soul to an unseelie fae. Whatever for?"

Whatever for, indeed. Why the hell was Merritt doing this? "Merritt," Ivy said urgently.

"The police are on their way," he replied. "Peters sent for them after the first gunshot."

"But…"

"There's a method to my madness, love," he said. "Please trust me on this."

Her breath caught at the word, love. "All right," she whispered.

"Penright and I were friends," McCann said, voice shaking as he looked at the medium's corpse. Bloodstains pooled on the carpet. "Edwin wasn't the only one to embrace magic for business purposes." He stomped the distance to the body, then rustled around Penright's robe, removing a slim glass tube similar to the one that held

Claudia. He couldn't read its label, but instinctively, Merritt knew what it was.

"Do the right thing," Merritt said wearily. "Let me release Edwin Thaddeus's spirit."

"I should throw it in a lake." McCann sounded as if he was near tears. "For the grief all of you have caused me, the sheer amount of money I've lost out on because Edwin's bitch of a wife wouldn't cooperate. Edwin deserves to spend the rest of eternity locked away!"

Claudia pushed herself up and started crawling toward McCann. Ezra was faster, knocking the tube out of his hand, then smashing it against the tabletop.

"Damn it!" snarled McCann.

All of them watched in morbid fascination as a silvery cloud formed out of the broken tube, suspended in the air for a few seconds. Before Merritt could blink, it zipped to McCann, melting into him. "Oh, my God," Merritt whispered.

McCann doubled over, coughing. He slowly straightened, eyes blinking in surprise, then looked at his hands. "Ezra?" he said in wonder. His voice was that of McCann's, but softer, more gentle.

The remaining color drained from Ezra's face. "Father?"

"My boy. Come here." He held out his arms. Ezra hesitated for half a second, then embraced McCann.

"Is that Edwin?" Ivy whispered. Her eyes were wide with shock and she looked as if she might faint.

At the sound of her voice, he turned to her. "Ivy?"

"Edwin!" She put a hand over her mouth and took a few steps toward McCann. Swaying on his feet, McCann put one of his arms around Ivy, then held her and Ezra. Ezra's shoulders shook with sobs.

"I can't stay long," McCann said. "I will be here long

enough to let the police arrest me for murder, and then I'll confess to my own before I leave Roger's body." He tightened his hold on them.

"Not even for a day or two?" Ezra said.

"I don't want to stay on this plane. It isn't natural."

From the floor, Claudia sniffled.

"You've freed my soul," Dr. Thaddeus said to Ezra. "I will never be able to thank you enough for that."

Shouts and footsteps sounded from somewhere in the house. Ivy stepped away, her eyes wet. "They're coming," she said.

"I know." Dr. Thaddeus kissed the top of Ezra's head like he was a little boy, then squeezed him in a final hug. "You'd best stand aside when the police arrive. I'll try and contact you after I leave McCann's body, before I cross over. Ezra, I love you more than words can say."

Ezra reluctantly let go and brushed tears away from his eyes. "I love you, Father."

"I'm proud of you both," Dr. Thaddeus said. "I love you both, too."

The door burst open. Dr. Thaddeus held up McCann's hands at the sight of the policemen, their weapons drawn. "Hello, gentleman," he said cheerfully. "I murdered Dr. Edwin Thaddeus with hemlock tea I gave him as a gift, and Mr. Penright with that gun. Hell of a way to go!"

IT WAS past midnight when Merritt, Ivy, Ezra, and Claudia crammed themselves into Merritt's ornithopter for the journey back to Ezra's flat. Ezra was silent the entire trip and sat on the passenger basket's floor with Claudia, letting her hold him. Ivy sniffled a time or two and didn't let go of Merritt's arm. She needed his strength right now, his quiet determination. "We still have to free the souls at the museum," she said.

"I will do that in the morning."

"Why not tonight?"

"Edwin said he would contact us tonight, if he could."

She'd nearly forgotten that part, so overwhelming and exhausting had the evening been. "Of course."

She'd spoken to her late husband tonight, something she'd never expected to do again. He'd been so eager to leave the mortal plane, desperate to get away. She thought about the other ghost that she hadn't seen. Then she glanced behind her at one who had appeared in flesh and blood tonight. "Who did you speak to earlier tonight? Before everything went to hell?"

"Penright's dead and McCann has been possessed to confess to murder, so it wasn't an unsuccessful evening." Despite the flippancy in his voice, Ivy heard pain there. Penright had tried to kill him, too, and nearly did so.

"Merritt…"

"I spoke to McCann's late wife. She was forced to return to the mortal plane in one of Penright's unseelie fae experiments. She's since returned to the afterlife now that Penright's dead." The ornithopter dipped a little to the side from a small gust of wind. Claudia shrieked from behind them.

"What about Claudia?" Ivy whispered in Merritt's ear.

"I don't know about Claudia." He took one hand off the ornithopter's controls to scrub his hand over his face. "I don't fucking know about her or how Penright resurrected her. It must have been something similar to that resurrection spell she translated for us." The one that didn't require a fresh corpse for a ghost to return to. He tossed a glance over his shoulder at Claudia, still huddled on the basket floor with Ezra. Ivy didn't know who was clinging more tightly to who.

Merritt landed the craft in Ezra's front garden, which didn't go unnoticed by him. "You'll move this tomorrow?" he asked Merritt. "I don't care, but my neighbors will."

"I'll move it tomorrow," Merritt promised.

Ezra fumbled with his key at the door, taking a couple of tries to unlock it. As soon as they stepped into the foyer, every light in the flat blazed on and Ivy thought she could feel a charge in the air. "Oh, God, what now?" said Ivy.

Merritt raised an eyebrow and shook off his coat. "I think Edwin has come by to visit."

A silence fell over them. After a few seconds, Ezra called, "Father?"

The lights flickered again. "He's here," Merritt said. "He's tired from possessing McCann and the pull of the afterlife is too much. He can't stay."

"Thank you for your help, Edwin," said Ivy over a lump in her throat. "Thank you for being my friend."

"I love you, Father," said Ezra softly.

The lights glowed again, so brightly that Merritt thought their glass bulbs might explode. "Your father says to check your sideboard," Merritt reported. "He has to leave now."

The lights went out, then returned a few seconds later at normal brightness. The air felt different, normal again, and Ivy knew that Edwin was truly gone.

Ezra rushed from the foyer to his parlor, returning with two sheets of paper. Face white, he handed one to Ivy. Written in pencil was a note:

*Thank you for your help in my life and death, Ivy. Be safe, be well, keep your magic close to you.*

Ivy brushed away tears as she read and re-read the

note. She couldn't imagine the strength it would have taken to write that as an incorporeal being.

Claudia couldn't do that, when she'd been a ghost for over a thousand years.

She glanced behind her at the former ghost, now sitting on the floor, bare feet in front of her. Ivy held out her hand.

Claudia considered it, then let Ivy help her to her feet. "Thank you," she said. She leaned against the wall. "I don't know how to exist in my body again." Her accent was muddied, almost flattened. She didn't sound English or like anyone Ivy had ever heard.

Ezra folded his letter and tucked it into his pocket. His eyes were red, but he looked calm, if tired and resigned. "Ezra?" Ivy said gently.

He shook his head. "He says he loves me and he's proud of me. He wished you and I could have been better friends before he died." His voice broke. "He's really gone." He held out his hand to Claudia. "Do you have somewhere to stay?"

She accepted it, letting him hold her to feet. "I don't know. I don't know why I'm still alive."

"What happened?" Merritt asked.

"Let's talk about this in the parlor," Ezra suggested. "I think all of us need to sit down." Like he was a gentleman leading a lady to the dance floor, he took Claudia's arm and led her, with her halting steps, to his parlor. She sank into the luxurious gray velvet sofa, sighing in relief.

"This is Claudia," Merritt said. "She's the ghost who haunted the flat across the corridor from mine."

Ezra nodded. "I can't believe I'm not surprised by this."

"Claudia, you've already met Ivy. This is Ezra Thaddeus, Ivy's stepson and Edwin Thaddeus's son."

"Long understood," Claudia replied.

"What happened?" Merritt asked. "How did this——" he gestured to her breathing corporeal form— "happen?"

"Penright appeared at your flat last night. He said a spell and unlocked the door. I stayed away from him, as you said, but he cast a spell that compelled me to him, then put me in a bottle." A visible shudder rippled through her at the memory. "It was like being buried alive. I could scream all I wanted but no one could hear me."

Merritt closed his eyes, and Ivy knew he was thinking about the spirits trapped in the museum.

"The spell he cast at that house was of a magic I've never heard of. The language pre-dated the Latin I spoke when I was alive the first time. Did you feel it?" She looked at each face in turn as if searching them. "It was a resurrection spell, some twist of unseelie magic and necromancy, I don't know."

"How do you feel?" Merritt pressed.

"This is my old body, or a copy of it. I know it, I'm not used to it anymore. I have to remember how to breathe. Walking is difficult. Even blinking is an effort." She looked at her hands in wonder, reminding Ivy of a baby discovering them. "I don't think I'm dying again. I've died before. This doesn't feel like it."

Ivy remembered Merritt telling her that Claudia never spoke about her death and rarely of her life in Londinium, nor how she made her way to Liverpool or when.

"I feel as if I've been sick for many years and have only just healed," Claudia continued. She sniffed. "It smells terrible in here, like something's burned."

Ezra colored. "I sometimes smoke in here."

"I can taste it." As if to illustrate her point, she made a face. To Merritt, she said, "I think I may actually be alive.

Do you know how long I could stay this way? The spell I read for you didn't have a way of reversing it."

"Do you want to stay this way?"

"I don't want to be killed again." Merritt flinched at her statement. Claudia herself looked surprised at it, as if she hadn't meant to blurt that out. "If I'm truly alive, I'd like to keep on being so. Do you know anyone who could say for sure?"

"Possibly my parents."

"They're welcome to visit, as soon as possible," Ezra said. "Claudia, you're welcome to stay here for the time being."

"Why can't I go back to the flat?" Claudia asked.

"The landlady wouldn't know you," Merritt said gently. "You couldn't stay in the flat you haunted."

"Why not?"

"Flats cost money. You have to pay rent."

"Oh. Of course." She looked dismayed, likely realizing that she knew nothing practical of the world she'd been haunting for hundreds, if not thousands of years. Ivy's heart ached for her, and judging from the look on Merritt's face, so did his.

"You can stay here," Ezra repeated. To Ivy and Merritt, he asked, "It's safe for you to return to the house and your flat, if you want."

Ivy had wanted that for weeks. She missed her home, feeling like she belonged somewhere, fiercely. She nodded.

"I'd like the company," Ezra added. "Especially from someone with Claudia's experience."

"Ezra," said Merritt, a touch of warning in his voice. "She's been through a great deal the last day and a half."

"I'm not going to pester her about it. It's just nice to have the company of someone who understands the paranormal, is all."

Ivy refrained from pointing out that she did, too. A witch for a stepmother wasn't the same as a resurrected Roman housemate who knew how ghosts and the afterlife worked.

"Are you sure you don't want us to stay tonight?" Merritt pressed. "You had a hell of a night." He didn't have to mention that Ezra had killed someone. Ivy didn't think she would ever forget the image of Penright crumpling to the floor, eyes wide open in surprise as he realized he'd been shot. It would haunt her nightmares for years to come.

Ezra looked undecided. "All right," he said. "Just for tonight. Claudia, do you mind sleeping on the sofa?"

"We could take the parlor," Ivy offered. Merritt nodded.

"I don't mind," Claudia replied. She bounced on the sofa cushions. "This is comfortable."

"I'll get a pillow and blankets." Ezra left before anyone else could speak.

"We'll talk more in the morning," Merritt promised Claudia. "We'll be down the hall, not far away. If you need anything or have any questions, you can wake us up."

Ezra returned with pillows, blankets stacked on top. "Let me show you about," he said. He held out his hand, and Claudia immediately let him help her up, then lean against him as she limped along. Her gait was a little stronger than it had been at McCann's house, as if she was remembering how to walk again.

Merritt put his hand on the small of Ivy's back and guided her away from the parlor. Once in their bedroom, he closed the door and faced her, as serious as he'd been back at the séance. "I have to tell you something."

Alarm flared through her. "What is it? Did you see Penright's ghost?"

"No, Penright isn't here. There aren't any ghosts here. It's something else, what I thought about when he tried to kill me. I felt myself dying, and I realized something." He looked away for a second, as if his news might be taken poorly.

Her heart thundered so loudly she thought he must be able to hear it hammering against her ribs. "What is it?"

"I'm in love with you, Ivy."

His words echoed in her mind for a moment. Her heartbeat slowed, her initial panic ebbing away as their impact hit her. "I thought about the same tonight. I didn't recognize it at first. I've never been in love before." Fresh tears welled in her eyes, but these ones weren't from terror or pain. "I knew you were special the moment you walked into my house."

"You ordered me to leave."

"I knew you'd return."

"It's the detective in me." He tucked an errant strand of hair behind her ear, tender gaze never leaving her face.

She leaned into him, needing his warmth and strength. She would for the rest of her days. "What happens next?"

His breath ruffled her hair. "Whatever we want."

*1 December, 1889*

*Dear Ivy and Merritt,*

*I'm truly in awe of your ability to shuck off all societal expectations with nary a care in the world. Your engagement announcement is not a surprise in and of itself. The announcement mere days after your mourning period ended is, but I suppose true love cannot wait.*

*I look forward to receiving an invitation to your wedding. I hope that wasn't too forward.*

*I hope you're enjoying your visit with the Langs, and that Spain is treating you well. Christmas must be infinitely more pleasant there than in dreary old England.*

*Your friend,*

*Ezra Thaddeus*

*P.S. Claudia is an exasperating, maddening housemate.*

# ABOUT THE AUTHOR

Jessica Marting is a sci-fi and paranormal romance author, art enthusiast (not quite an artist, despite all that time in art school), an avid reader, and makeup collector. She lives in Toronto.

For updates about books, giveaways, and other fun stuff, subscribe to her newsletter: jessicamarting.com/newsletter

## Magic & Mechanicals

*Wolf's Lady*

*Sea Change*

*Bound in Blood*

*Dragon's Keep*

*Spellbound*

## Zone Cyborgs

*Haven*

*Paradise*

*Oasis*

*Safe Harbor*

*Sanctuary*

*Refuge*

## The Commons

*Supernova*

*Celestial Chaos*

## Standalone Novels & Novellas

*Spindle's End*

*Trade Secrets*

*Neon Vice*

*Dead Ringer*

*Escape From Europa 10*

*Castaways*

*Demon's Favor*

*Rapture*